Maya,
Happy sleuthing.

SUNNY SIDE UP

Daniel Stallings

Daniel Stallings

Pace Press

Fresno, California

Sunny Side Up

Copyright © 2018 by Daniel Stallings. All rights reserved.

Cover design by Dominic Grijalva

Published by Pace Press
An imprint of Linden Publishing
2006 South Mary Street, Fresno, California 93721
(559) 233-6633 / (800) 345-4447
QuillDriverBooks.com

Pace Press and Colophon are trademarks of
Linden Publishing, Inc.

ISBN 978-1-61035-311-3

135798642

Printed in the United States of America
on acid-free paper.

Library of Congress Cataloging-in-Publication Data on file.

Contents

To Donna McCrohan Rosenthal
for making this all possible.

Thank you for everything.

CHAPTER 1

Port

"Johnson! Get your head out of your ass and fluff those orchids!"

Liam Johnson swallowed the urge to fling the little crystal urn at the maître d's face. Paul had a point. This wasn't the time to think about his late father. The cruise ship would depart in an hour. Li made a good show of fluffing the flowers, pulled the white tablecloth taut, and rearranged the place setting. Paul McCaffrey bellowed orders into Li's ear.

"You missed a spot on that dessert spoon! No, the brandy snifters go on the table, not the champagne flutes! That napkin isn't folded properly! Start over!"

Li's fingers trembled with each new order. Sweat peppered his sharply groomed black hair. Summoning his patience, he dispatched his duties with quick, cautious precision. Paul glowered at the table.

"It's a start," he said. "Now get moving! You have thirty tables to finish before we launch, and I'm being generous!" Despite the carpet on the floor, Paul's black patent-leather dress shoes pounded away as he stormed the breadth of the dining room. Li pushed a sigh from his throat and returned to the tables. Paul's thirty was Li's fifty. He maneuvered the cart laden with clattering flatware to the next stop. Tight, little stress lines— three years in the making—pulled against his mouth like puppet strings.

Paul's voice shattered the peace of the ship's dining room.

"I thought I told everyone that the champagne is for tray pass *only!* Get the flutes off the tables! Snifters! Do I have to repeat myself? Snifter, snifters, snifters!"

Li polished a gold-tinted fork and slipped into his thoughts.

Tomorrow...I can get through tomorrow. I'll just pretend nothing happened.

"These trays are disgusting! Get them washed this instant!"

I just won't think about Dad...or hospitals...or the fact we couldn't afford flowers for the memorial...

"No no NO! I TOLD you we're using the *gold*-rimmed plates for the amuse-bouche!"

I guess I can't think about Mom or Anna either...

"Johnson! Are you *still* working on that table?"

Shoving the memories aside, Li set three additional tables before Paul roared at him to polish the ice buckets. The passengers were boarding. In three hours, dinner would be served. Another cruise of bad manners, bad tips, and exemplary service would begin.

"Now don't miss a single speck, Johnson! I want these babies to sparkle! Get to work while I inspect your tables!"

Li shined the buckets, losing himself again in the jungle of his thoughts.

I wish I could have saved you, Dad...

"Christ, look at this mess! You only set four tables, and all of the flowers are off-center! You're just begging me to abandon you in Mexico, aren't you? Maybe you'll land a job as a tourist jockey in Ensenada! Finish those buckets and fix these tables!"

I'll fix something all right...I want to fix my rotten life...

"What are you doing, Johnson? Get your ass moving. NOW!"

Li scrubbed the silver finish with a rag, dismissing the whine of pain in his elbow. As he worked, he saw a blond flash reflected in the mirrored stomach of the bowl. He adjusted the ice bucket's position to get a better view.

Paul strode to the dining room entrance on the wings of his over-polished dress shoes. His face twinkled with a face-splitting smile.

"Mademoiselle Jackson!" he exclaimed in an accent that would insult any Parisian native. "Welcome back to my dining room! We have missed you on the Howard Line."

Charlegne Jackson closed her compact with a snap. Her eyes lounged behind huge designer sunglasses that looked a little too much like an insect's compound eye. "Thank you, Jean Paul. What are the seating arrangements for dinner?"

"As you know, Mademoiselle—"

"Spare me the flattery. Where am I sitting?"

"The Captain's Table, of course. Captain Crayle wouldn't dream of—"

"Steven and Priscilla will eat there, yes?"

"It has all been arranged."

"Who else is dining there?"

"Mademoiselle, I—"

"*Who else is dining there?*"

Paul flinched as if her words bit him. The accent and the airs evaporated.

"R-Rosemary Hale, Miss Jackson."

Charlegne pushed her shades onto the top of her golden head. Her eyes whittled into thin slots of blue fire, like the gas rings on a stove. Her lipsticked mouth tightened into a frown. Reopening her compact and applying a thin, ivory veil to her smooth face, she said, "Be sure that Rosie and I are seated at opposite ends of the table, Jean Paul. I don't need a repeat of Fashion Week. Do you understand?"

"Yes, Miss Jackson."

"Good. I drink only Dom Pérignon Rosé 2000. See to it that I have a chilled bottle adjacent to my seat."

"Yes, Miss Jackson."

"Who's that boy over there?"

Li's heart jammed into his throat. She pointed directly at him. He bent over the ice bucket and burnished the metal until his fingers cramped.

"Liam?" Paul asked. "He's just a waiter. No one important. No one notices him." He dismissed the thought with a flick of his hand. "If you want him fired..."

Li winced.

"I want him at the table tonight."

"You can't be serious!"

"Jean Paul, do it."

"But Miss Jackson—!"

"Jean Paul, you know I don't like interruptions. He will be my server tonight. No further discussion." The compact snapped shut, and she sailed away.

Paul rounded on Li. "Get the damn Rosé, Johnson! If Chef Will has a problem with it, send him to me! Charlegne Jackson will roast us alive if she doesn't have her Dom! GET GOING!"

Li sprinted off after the word "damn." He moved so fast that he collided into a coworker pushing another cart. Dinnerware crashed to the ground in a shrill orgy.

"Christ, Johnson! Can't you focus for once? Forget the Dom! I'll do it! Get out of this dining room and don't come back until service! If Charlegne didn't specifically request for you, I would have thrown you overboard! GET OUT!"

Charlegne swept like an albatross down the passageway encircling the Grand Atrium, crew members ducking and diving out of her way. Her objective was the elevator. A mouse of a woman yapped at her elbow.

"Oh, I love the Howard Line! Glamorous to perfection!" Priscilla Reilly chirped. "Not even the Waldorf could match this ship!"

"The Waldorf has better linens."

"And the service is strictly professional. We won't have to worry about any inappropriate behavior on this trip. That steward on the Royal Meridian Line disgusted me."

The women mounted the glass-paneled elevator, zooming upward, the Atrium stretching into a nonsensical blur. Priscilla's praise bulldozed over any canned music they may have heard. "And the maître d' treats every guest like royalty…"

Charlegne rechecked her complexion. "Jean Paul flatters too much. He could benefit from swapping his tongue for extra shoe polish."

"He's such a charming man. And such a funny little accent."

"Yes. A Parisian transplanted from Orange County, I shouldn't wonder."

Priscilla twittered in her wilted cabbage dress. "Oh Charlegne! Jean Paul is the most discreet—"

"*Please* tell me Steven is on the Sports Deck, Priscilla." Charlegne's voice strained in her throat. She rubbed her right temple.

"Oh yes, he is! He went up there after you went into the dining room. He said he—"

"Good. I'm getting a headache." She opened her Birkin and fished out a bottle of pills, popping two in her mouth like they were peppermints. "I want it understood, I need my rest, Priscilla. Take my phone. Handle that business with *Harper's*. I intend to spend the afternoon in peace."

"Yes, of course, Charlegne! Do you still want to approve the dress?"

"Must you bother me with questions?"

"I didn't mean to bother you, naturally! I'm so sorry..."

"Use the shirt dress. Look #27. The rest is immaterial."

Charlegne and Priscilla stepped out of the elevator and pushed through a set of double doors, across the passageway. Sunshine rushed their eyes, saltwater perfumed the air. Sea birds roosted on the white railing circling the deck.

"Hello, Stevie!" Charlegne's voice rang out with an icy bite. "Good Lord! Aren't you *melting* in that ridiculous getup? It must be a hundred degrees out here!"

Leaning on the railing, Steven Danforth tugged at the collar of his three-piece suit. "You're late, Charlegne."

"I saw to an irritating little matter in the ship's dining room. Rosie Hale is on this cruise."

Steven stopped wiping the sweat off his brow and stared at his client. "Rosie? She tried to strangle you at Fashion Week last year. Why is she here?"

"To accomplish her twisted revenge fantasy, of course. She's on vacation, Stevie! Why else would she be on a cruise?"

"Take it easy, Charlegne."

"Shut up, Stevie." For the fourth time, Charlegne examined her face in her compact. "Damn these wrinkles...don't they ever go away?"

"Maybe if you stopped scowling so much."

A gull shrieked overhead. A smirk tweaked Charlegne's lips, and her eyes gleamed with malice. "But then how would you know what I was thinking, Stevie?"

Steven said nothing.

"Priscilla, get my beach bag from my cabin. I'm going to sunbathe." Once the assistant scuttled off, Charlegne turned to her business manager. "Are you going to stay and watch, Stevie dear?" She undid the tie on her wrap dress.

"I think I'd rather watch seagull poop dry on the railings."

"Hardly a fair trade." The fabric slipped off her shoulders.

"Better yet, I think I'd rather watch Priscilla sunbathe."

Charlegne's lips curved into a prim smile. "She'd be flattered, I'm sure." The dress collapsed to her feet like a dead skin.

Steven rolled his eyes and banished the sweat from his forehead, again. "You, on the other hand, are a disgusting exhibitionist."

Charlegne smoothed out her one-piece bathing suit. "And you are a fussy old Puritan." She snapped her fingers, a crisp sound like a twig breaking. A deck attendant materialized at her side. "Take this." She tossed her dress at him. "Stevie, tell Priscilla I'll be on the Sunbathing Deck. And remind her that I do not care how this ship is like The Ritz, The Savoy, or the damn *Love Boat*. I'm going to grind sleeping pills and put them in her coffee if she keeps it up."

"You make a wonderful boss, Charlegne."

She shook loose the curls of her golden hair and adjusted her insect-eye shades. "And don't you forget it, honey. *La Charlegne* has done more for you than you'd like to admit. Wouldn't you like to keep it that way, Stevie?" She strode off, the attendant doing all he could to keep up.

Steven said nothing. His hands were balled into fists.

CHAPTER 2

"I Miss No One"

Shoulders hunched and eyes glued to his feet, Li shuffled out of the room before Paul started throwing steak knives. He trudged toward the Temptations Lounge directly across from the dining room. He knew Travis would be working on the inventory.

As Li entered the red, black, and chrome lounge, Travis stocked bottles of whiskey and vermouth onto the glass shelves behind the bar, whistling a bright work song that grated against Li's growing depression.

"So, has Paulie learned to swear at you in French yet?" the bartender asked without turning. Li plopped onto a barstool and buried his face in his arms.

"How did you know it was me?" Li asked, his voice muffled through his pretzel of shame.

"Dude, I could hear Paulie shriek from here. You must have really set him off."

"Why does he hate me so much?"

"Why is the sky blue? Paulie hates everyone. You can't let him get to you, Li."

"I'm trying not to, but my mind just isn't cooperating."

"It's the anniversary of your dad's death, isn't it?"

Li's face shot up, and his smoky blue eyes swam in little lakes. He sank back into the nest his arms made. "That's tomorrow."

"I thought so. You always get so depressed around this time. He died three years ago. You can't change that."

"I know...I don't need someone to tell me."

Travis heaved a box of vodka bottles onto the counter and began to sift through it like he was at a garage sale. "You don't need to get snotty, Li. I'm just trying to help. I'd ply you with Smirnoff but you're too young, and like you, I need this job."

"At least you don't have a boss twisting a knife into your back."

"Hey, I'm just waiting until the lottery supplements my wild and crazy bachelor lifestyle." He reached into his shirt pocket, removed three tickets, and kissed them with a flourish. "Come on, baby. Daddy wants a Corvette."

"Daddy needs to finish inventory before our thirsty travelers resort to drinking pool water," Li remarked.

Lifting two bottles of vodka, Travis turned back to the shelves. "If they do, I'll be there with a camera and *The National Enquirer* on line one."

He resumed whistling, his notes like needles in Li's ears. Li feared for the safety of the stemware.

"Li," Travis said, "the reason Paulie hates you is because you're the new kid. And Mr. Phony-ass Frenchman despises training newbies. I'm just happy he doesn't swear in that stupid accent. If I hear even one *le ass*, I am downing a whole bottle of tequila and throwing up on those shiny shoes."

Li snorted with laughter, clamping his hands over his mouth to smother the giggles. Travis grinned, puffed out his chest, and smoothed back his ship-shape crew cut. Li laughed harder.

"Glad to know I can still get you to laugh, Li. You've been such a downer, lately. I can see those stress lines forming around your mouth. It's a shame to see them in such a young guy..."

Li's gaze dropped to the ebony countertop, and he drew looping spirals on it with his finger. Little crow's feet crinkled in the corners of his eyes. "Did you know that Charlegne Jackson is on this cruise?"

Travis resumed stocking the shelves. "Ah, so the Ice Queen returneth. I wondered why I felt a chill."

"She wants me to be the server at the Captain's Table."

"And Paulie's going to let you get away with that? Hmmm...might be a good time to cause some serious damage. Give 'em hell, Liam!"

Li's gaze shifted to a painting of a mere suggestion of a woman wrapped in red veils. "Why did she ask for me though?"

"Why shouldn't she?"

"I'm just a kid."

"Twenty is hardly a baby, Li." He began cleaning the glass tumblers. "My guess is that she just wanted someone invisible. You're the most nondescript guy on this ship."

Li's head swung back to face his friend. The little lines around his lips deepened. "I'm a nobody, then. Is that it?"

"I never said that, Li."

"You practically did."

"Why on earth are you fighting me all of a sudden?"

Li deflated. Wrinkles scored his face. "I'm just exhausted."

"Maybe you should stay home. You're going to wear yourself out. I'm sure Paulie would be more than happy to let you off."

"This isn't a joke, Travis! I need the money! They shut the power off last month because I couldn't afford to pay the bill." Li's face burrowed into his hands.

Travis set down a tumbler and clapped a hand on Li's shoulder. "Hey now...You're falling apart...I think it's time you go back home."

"No...I can't." Li gently shook off his friend's grip. "Dad wasn't a quitter. Even after everything collapsed on top of him, he fought like the tough old sailor he was."

"You're not like him, Li."

"I'm his son. That's better than nothing." He pounded the countertop with his fist.

Travis chuckled and twisted his polishing rag into a rope. "Atta boy!" He whacked his friend on the shoulder with the rag. "Now are you going to go in there and show Paulie that you aren't a screw-up?"

Li's eyes widened. "Are you nuts? Paul would filet me and serve me as the main course if I went in there now."

Travis laughed again. "Good. Just making sure you haven't abandoned your sanity. Now what's this about Ms. Hoity Toity coming on this cruise?"

"Is she really as stuck-up as you paint her, Travis?"

"Oh, right...You haven't had the 'honor' of serving our resident princess." He started to wipe the counter down. "Charlegne will straighten you out. She has Paulie and these two stooges of hers horse-whipped. Hell, she might even have you prancing after her like a little puppy in no time. You would think a fashion designer would act more like an introverted, artsy-fartsy type, but not the 'elegant' Miss Jackson! Oh no! God forbid! You'd think she shits gold bricks!"

He punctuated his remark by tossing the duster onto the counter and folding his arms. Li suppressed a knowing smile.

"Someone knows her a little more intimately than he's letting on."

"Oh, I'll admit it. I had pictures of the woman stashed in the bottom of my sock drawer when I was in high school. I had no problem moaning naughty words to her. You probably don't remember her *Vogue* spread fifteen years ago. That baby was my *Playboy* for months. Ever see her modeling shots?"

Li shook his head. "I know her name and that's it."

"If your hormones ever get the better of you, I suggest hitting up any magazine stand from here to New Jersey."

"What happened? Why are you so critical?"

"I got to meet her on the ship. Wet dreams should never talk, in my opinion. I've had warmer receptions from a snowman." He continued to buff the counter. "Then there are her special 'requests.' During my first cruise with her, she downed chardonnay as if it was water. Two years ago, she drank nothing but Perrier. I'm waiting for her to demand gin and laxatives."

"Your drink memory is almost as impressive as your wit. Ever think about going into stand-up?"

"But then where else would I see rich people getting wasted?"

A voice exploded in the passageway.

"You are a smarmy son of a bitch! Get rid of that stupid accent and lift a damn finger for a change! Come on, Sally!"

A hurricane of a man blustered through the door of the lounge, the force of his entrance causing the painting to swing on its perch. A quivering shell of a woman hiding under a cowl of pale hair tiptoed after him.

"You there!" the man bellowed. "Bar jockey! When is this damn thing open?"

"After dinner, sir," Travis replied, polishing the bar taps. "Eight o'clock."

"I have to wait until then?"

"Ship policy."

"Do you know who I am? I could sue you all from here to Sunday!"

"I'm sorry, sir, but those are the rules."

The woman crept forward. "Aaron, honey..."

"Shut up, Sally! I'm not letting some beer-slinging punk tell ME when I can and can't drink! Here!" He slammed a couple of fifties onto the countertop. "Tell the stewards to bring a bottle of your best Scotch to my cabin, Aaron Brent. WITH AN APOLOGY FOR DENYING ME SERVICE!"

Aaron grabbed his wife's wrist and dragged her toward the door.

Travis exhaled. "I would kill to be you, Li. He didn't even notice you sitting there. Then again, Paulie is going to send you to their table first chance he gets. Hope you have good health insurance."

Li didn't respond. His gaze lingered on the woman being hauled away by her husband. She managed to glance back, her eyes wide and frightened. Something about those eyes...

Li had seen Sally Brent's face somewhere before.

Charlegne dipped her toes into the swimming pool and drew wide, lazy whirlpools in the water. She sat alone on the tiled edge like a mermaid, her eyes locked on the western horizon. Sinking sunlight warmed her hair from ice blond to a rich, honey gold. Sunsets were not her priority. Her mind filled the empty space with the faces of the passengers who had left the deck, faces she would be unable to forget. She couldn't get rid of them. She began appraising those figures haunting her, an idle distraction from her more...unwelcome memories.

The fat woman in that hideous one-piece is going to wear a "form-fitting" dress at dinner. I just know it. She'll be squeezed into it like a pear in a rubber glove. I bet it'll be in a disgusting shade of neon. No...White. She's just the sort who would throw on a big, white parachute of a gown and believe she's Karolina Kurkova. In an hour, I'll finally learn what ship's sails do to the human figure.

A shadow draped over her shoulder and, without turning, she spoke to the newcomer.

"Hello, Captain."

"I guess I'll never learn how you do that, Charlegne," Captain Crayle replied, his voice deep, smooth, and tinged with the grit of world experience. *Like my father's,* Charlegne thought.

"Do you expect me to reveal all of my secrets, Johnnie?" She glanced over her shoulder at the figure in starched whites blazing against the backdrop of the golden-lit ship.

"Do you have any other secrets, Charlegne?"

"Why? Are you writing my biography? Shouldn't I be dead before that happens?" She kicked a few drops of pool water into the air and watched gravity take them home again.

"Is something wrong, Charlegne?"

Why can't everyone leave me alone? "No."

"You know if something's—"

"I said no, Jonathon."

"So I heard." Charlegne heard Captain Crayle's footsteps advance toward her, but she hardened her sights on the horizon, squinting against the encroaching sunset. "You weren't thinking about...us, were you?"

"There was never an 'us'."

"There could have been."

"There could have been many things. A relationship was not one of them."

"Not even after that night in Alhambra?"

Charlegne's shoulders stiffened. "A lot of things happened that night, but it was all tempered by a healthy flood of whiskey. In fact, it's almost like that night never happened at all. I certainly don't remember anything. Do you?"

Captain Crayle unburdened himself with a sigh. "I guess you're not one for reminiscing."

"Memories kill. I refuse to have any. This trip will remain nothing more than a stress relief. A big, seaworthy Valium."

"Got a wish to see Mexico?"

She waved away the question. "Just trying to get away for a while."

"Away?"

Of all the lousy... "Yes, away. I had a busy spring season. I had Priscilla make time for me. If anyone can keep people from bothering me, it's her." Her mouth twitched into a wry smile. "That's the thing I love about Priscilla. She has a marvelous gift for making people uncomfortable."

"But not you?"

Charlegne turned to the captain, the smile still hovering on her lips. She was far away in her unwanted memories. Sunlight glimmered on the surface of the pool, giving her a golden, sequined backdrop. "I am far too wounded to let anything get under my skin."

She returned to the sunset. The captain rested a hand on her shoulder, and she turned instinctively toward his touch. His fingers felt warm against her cheek.

"You miss him, don't you?"

She began picking at the fabric of her beach bag, tearing a small hole in it with her fingernails. "I miss no one."

CHAPTER 3

Ice and Fire

"You've been crying."

Charlegne's hand stopped mid-brush. Patches of caked-on foundation creased around her eyelids. Reflected in her dressing table mirror, she saw a tuxedo-clad Steven Danforth leaning against the door. Her hand began to tremble.

I refuse to turn around, she thought. *I refuse!*

"I have no idea what you're talking about, Steven."

He made a show of examining a spot on his lapel. "You called me Steven."

"That's your name, isn't it?"

"You only call me Steven when you are upset."

"Upset...or pissed. Let's not forget that."

Steven crossed to the nightstand and fingered through the pages of a magazine. "No...it would be silly to forget that, wouldn't it? Pretty little Charlegne in her ivory tower never forgets, does she? She's still trapped in the past."

Tiny breaths of rouge puffed off the quivering bristles of her makeup brush. "Why are you saying such stupid things?"

"Why do you have this *Vogue* from fifteen years ago? That was the last time you modeled for them, right?"

I hate you, Steven. "Didn't your mother ever tell you it's impolite to look through a woman's belongings?"

"So, you won't tell me why you have it?"

"Your interest in my business is starting to get too personal. Need I remind you that I am the one who signs the checks?"

"You're trying to take control again."

You're damn right, I am. "Go away, Steven. I'm trying to concentrate."

"Trying to cover up your swollen eyes?"

"You've always had a difficult time understanding the words 'go away.'"

Her business manager strolled to her chair and pulled a curl of blond hair out of the chignon she wore, letting the lock dangle in front of her eyes. "You look prettier this way."

Charlegne swiped the loose strand back. "Don't tell me what looks good, Steven. I've made a career of looking good. I don't need your damn opinion."

"You may not 'need' it, but I have a feeling you want it."

"Leave me alone. Get out, or I'll fire you."

"Threaten all you want, Charlegne. I know who you'll come running to when you finally break."

I'd kill myself first. "I don't like using the word 'please,' Steven. Get. Out. Now."

Steven plucked a small ring out of the lacquered jewelry box sitting on the dressing table. The diamond looked like a speck of dust. "Will you wear this tonight?"

The brush fell from her hand and clattered on the tabletop. To Charlegne, it sounded like an explosion in her heart.

Rosemary Hale nearly tore her hair out by the roots, as she twisted the fiery mane into a haphazard bun. Her teeth creaked and cracked against each other. She felt a distant urge to punch her reflection.

Oh that bitch, she thought, *I am going to rip off all her hair and shove it down her throat! I knew she was going to be here! I just knew it!*

"Damn that selfish whore," she muttered. "Damn her straight to hell."

"What was that, darling?" On the edge of her vision, she saw her husband's eyes crest the horizon of the onboard newsletter like little chestnut suns.

"That stupid, self-centered cow just had to come on our cruise."

She heard pages ruffling. "Don't start on that again, Rosie."

"I'll start it if I want to! She always does this! Any time I go away to relax, she's there with her prissy, self-entitled manners and her buzzing flock of airheads! Did you see that woman following her around? My God! I don't think I could muster the patience to endure THAT every single day!"

"Patience was never one of your virtues, dear."

Rosemary swung around in her seat and clasped her husband's hands, crumpling the newsletter. "Marty, is there any way we can get off this ship? I can't stand being in the same country with her, let alone having to sit with her at dinner."

"Darling..."

"If only she was ugly...if only the years had been as cruel to her as they've been to me...I might be able to look her in the face. But no...she just sits there, all gorgeous and loved with the jewels and the champagne and the limousines. Everyone is oblivious to how much of a bitch she is! I'm going to punch her teeth out and turn her into the disgusting, tooth-less hag she deserves to be! Isn't that how they did it in *Snow White and the Seven Dwarves?*"

Her husband pulled his hands out of hers and resumed reading. "So what if she's beautiful?"

Rosemary's breathing quickened. Her chest rose and fell in short, sharp bursts like a piston in an engine. "Out of all that, the only thing you pick up on IS THE FACT SHE'S BEAUTIFUL?"

"Rosie...dear..."

"Don't call me 'dear' unless you mean it, Martin!"

"I do mean it."

Her eyes sharpened into tight slits. "You know I despise Charlegne..."

Martin leveled his gaze with hers. "And yet, you're going to let her run your life."

"What do you mean?"

"What other meaning could I have? It's been fifteen years."

Oh, no...Oh, hell no...He can't say it. She returned to her aggressive hair-styling. "I loathe that number."

"The number stands. You need to get over it."

Rosemary pursed her lips into a tight knot. She bit the tip of her tongue. She heard the impatient snap of the newsletter.

"I'm starting to think that you enjoy being angry, Rosie."

Maybe I do. "That's stupid. Why would I do that?"

"I don't think I need to answer that question."

"Then you have no need to criticize how I feel about a certain murdering bitch."

"She didn't kill anyone."

Rosemary's eyes drilled into the smooth silver of the mirror. She imagined Charlegne, dressed in summer white, perfect like a Dresden china doll, shoving a man off a bridge. "She practically did."

"Rosie—"

"Shut up, Martin." *I'd sooner die than think about him.* She jammed bangle after bangle onto her wrist, stacking them like fat, silver shackles. "If I can get through this god-awful dinner without strangling her."

A hand slipped one of the bracelets off her wrist while another warmed her bare shoulder. She felt her husband rest his chin on the curve of her neck and kiss her earlobe.

"Darling—"

"Shut up, Martin. Don't say anything."

"You have to learn that—"

"Finish that sentence and I call the attorney." Her knuckles popped as she tightened her fingers into fists.

"It's going to kill you."

"Stop it, Martin. Stop it, right now. You know I want to explode if I hear his name."

"You really need to settle down, Rosie."

"Marty, she makes it so difficult!"

"You make it difficult. You're the one holding on to this grudge about Dustin."

He said it...Oh God, HE SAID IT! Rosemary shoved her husband away, her fingers curved like claws. Her hastily bundled hair sprang into a confusion of loose red curls, like a volcano retching lava. But she didn't explode. Her body stiffened, trembled, the tension making her skin burn white-hot. Her eyes, green as dragon hide, gleamed.

"Grudge?" she asked, keeping her tone low and even. "You think I'm carrying something as shallow as a grudge against Charlegne? Let me remind you what she did, honey." Her voice quivered. Little earthquakes. "She lied to my baby brother. She said she loved him. Dustin adored her. Then the bitch left him for another man." Her words scraped her throat. "So Dustin jack-knifed off a bridge into a river!" Salty tears stung her eyes. "She killed him. Charlegne murdered Dustin, as if she pushed him herself. He committed suicide because of her. She drove him to it. Dustin was one of the few people left in my family. Do you know what it's like to watch as your whole family is gradually slaughtered around you?" She wiped away her tears, smearing her makeup. "I hate her. God, I hate her. I live in constant fear that she's going to take another person I love from me. Why do you think I moved from Los Angeles? I've had enough tragedy this year alone to haunt my nightmares until I die. Oh Marty..." She seized the lapels of his dinner jacket and pulled him toward her. "Can we please cancel the trip? Every time I see that woman, I want to beat her ugly face in. I can't do this, Marty...I just can't."

"So, Charlegne wins again." Martin disconnected her grip on his jacket and straightened his lapels. "Honestly, Rosie, aren't you tired of the constant hate?"

Rosemary held her tongue, turning back to see if she still wanted to right hook her reflection. The image of Charlegne danced across her mind.

"I see. You're going hold onto that grudge until it eats away your soul. I'm sorry, but I don't enjoy watching that happen to my wife."

Martin tossed the newsletter onto the dressing table. Rosemary watched it blanket her jewelry box like a coffin lid.

"Finish up, Rosie. We're going to be late for dinner. Put on your happy face, dear. The staff doesn't need an encore of Fashion Week."

Rosemary pinched her lips into a taut line. She picked up the newsletter and smoothed it out on the tabletop.

This is the skin on her face...

She tore the paper into strips.

CHAPTER 4

Dinner

"I don't speak French, dammit! What the hell is chatter-bree-and aww poyver anyway?"

Aaron Brent tossed his menu across the table. It collided with the freshly fluffed orchids and upset the whole arrangement. Li stood next to the table, rocking on one leg and biting his lower lip. He lost the feeling in his toes.

"*Chateaubriand au poivre*," Li replied. "It's a classic dish. Filet mignon crusted in black peppercorns..." Aaron's face swelled purple with frustration. "It's a steak."

"HA! I'll be the judge of THAT! Get it and make sure it's medium! I don't like my meat bloody! If there's even a spot of blood, it's your ass, kid!"

"Yes, sir. And what will you have, madam?"

Sally flinched. Her blond hair hung around her face in a limp, dirty curtain. She mumbled, but the French flowed smoothly from her lips. "*Lapin et chasseur.*"

Rabbit, Li thought. *It fits.*

Li straightened the toppled centerpiece, gathered the menus, and sped across the dining room. Paul, now consumed in his role of Jean Paul, directed the waiters, hissing orders in their ears as they passed.

"Get the lead out, Johnson! Charlegne will be here any second, and if she doesn't see you at her table, it will be your neck on the line!"

Li raced into the kitchen. Executive Chef William Laurence expedited the service, his belly clogging the pass-through like a huge cork. Spouts of fire growled among the many white coats attending them. The chef's voice bashed against the normal kitchen noise. "Filet mid-rare! Two trout! Two lamb medium! Salmon tartare! I can't wait all day!"

With the Brents' order delivered, Li hustled into the dining room and plowed toward the Captain's Table. His feet protested in his too-small dress shoes.

"What took you so long, Johnson?" Paul hissed. "Did you come by dog sled? Get your ass over to Rosemary Hale's chair and pull it out! Christ, it's like I have to train you all over again!"

Li did so. Rosemary thanked him and turned her attention to the sommelier who was offering a wide selection of expensive Pinots. He saw taut wrinkles pull against her lips. They were sisters to his own.

"So what's the best grub on the menu anyway?" Rosemary asked.

Her question went unanswered. The guests' attention was arrested by the entrance of Charlegne Jackson, easily cast as Aphrodite dressed in moonlight for a classical painting. Sheer silver silk swirled around her lithe figure. Rosemary turned around, and Li saw a fist form at the end of her bangle-choked forearm. To him, the bracelets formed an iron gauntlet. Paul grazed Li's shoulder as he swept to Charlegne's side, his shoes competing with the luster of her gown.

"Mademoiselle Jackson," he said, "you look divine this evening! Like a goddess!"

"Show me to my seat, Jean Paul."

"Naturally, mademoiselle." He elbowed Li out of the way, pulling out the seat at the head of the table. Charlegne sank into her chair, keeping her glare locked on Rosemary's face. Her two compatriots flanked her.

"It's been a long time, Rosie dear," she said.

Rosemary's eyes narrowed. "Not long enough, Charlegne."

The sommelier poured the Rosé into a champagne flute, the sole one on the table. Charlegne cut him off with sharp flick of her hand. "It always seems like that, doesn't it? Tragedies from a dozen years ago can hurt as badly as if they happened yesterday."

Rosemary ordered a stiff brandy. "Becoming a philosopher in your old age, Charlegne?"

"It's the only entertainment I have, I suppose. I don't have a family to run back to like you, dear."

"You mean the family YOU destroyed?"

Charlegne unleashed a cold smile. "Anything you lost isn't nearly as bad as what I lost, Rosie." She drained her champagne.

Rosemary's teeth buried themselves in her lower lip. Her half-tamed mane of hair bristled with latent electricity. Martin Hale quickly took his wife's hand and stroked it.

Paul whispered to his subordinate. "Go away and tell Chef Will to fire the first course while I handle the amuse-bouche and the menu."

Li turned on his heel and swept into the kitchen. Chef Will barked at him the second the double doors parted.

"Johnson! You're a minute late! This will ruin our turnaround if you keep this up! Your entrées for table forty-six are ready."

"Fire the first course for Table 50 V.I.P." Li didn't bother to address the critique of his work ethic.

"Oh? So, Her Majesty finally showed up for dinner, eh? Very well. I'll need eight tartares ready to fly, boys! We'll be serving the soup tableside in the silver tureen. Get moving!"

Li grabbed the two entrées and sped to the Brents' table.

"There you are!" Aaron roared. "I've been near starvation! What kind of dining room are you running here?"

"Apologies for the delay, sir." Li set the dinners down. Aaron poked his steak with a sausage of a finger.

"It's COLD! If I wanted cold meat, I would have eaten a ham sandwich! Take this back immediately!"

Li bit his lip. "Right away, sir. I'm sorry for the inconvenience."

The chef glowered at Li when he returned. "COLD? What did you do, boy? Now our timing is thrown off! Jack! Refire a filet! Medium! And this time Johnson, don't be late!"

"Yes, sir." Li scuttled away with the appetizer-filled cart.

"Johnson!" Paul snarled. "Have you been napping? Charlegne and Rosemary are going to kill each other if we don't get food in their mouths and shut them up! Serve them NOW!"

Li scattered the salmon tartares around the table, and appreciative forks removed appetizing morsels. Then it was back to the kitchen for Mr. Brent's entrée.

"Here, Johnson! Piping hot. Whatever you did before, don't do it again! And get back here in time for the soup course!"

"You call this medium? This is practically burnt! Did you roast it over an open flame? I guess I have to order it medium rare just to get it cooked properly! Take it back!"

Li's feet swelled in his shoes.

"Overcooked? I've never seen a more beautiful medium in my life! Fine then. Jack! Re-refire the filet! Mid-rare this time! And Johnson, get your butt moving to Table 50 for the soup course. It's been five minutes since the appetizers went out."

The tureen glistened under the crystal-drunk chandeliers as Li wheeled it to the table. He ladled lobster bisque into eager bowls while Paul growled at him.

"You are making us look horrible to Charlegne! Where have you been? She asked specifically for you, and it takes you eons to show up!"

Back to the kitchen. "We're carving the roast tableside, Johnson. You'll be handling the jus. Here's your steak. See if you can get the guy to actually eat it for a change!"

"Blech! There's too much pepper in this dish! It's like licking a pepper mill! Take it back!"

"Too much pepper? On steak *au poivre*? This man wouldn't know the difference between *béchamel* and *tomate!*"

"I swear you are the slowest server in this dining room, Johnson! Clear these bowls and refill Charlegne's Rosé!"

Oh please stop, Li thought. *Please stop yelling at me...*

"Here's the damn steak, Johnson! Dump it on his table and get back here immediately for the lamb course!"

Li's ankles started to rebel.

"I suppose this will have to do since none of you can pull your heads out of your asses. But don't expect a tip from ME, kid! You're lucky I haven't notified your superior."

"The jus is getting cold, Johnson! Are you incapable of showing up on time? Jack! Luis! Carry the lamb on that mirrored platter! Johnson, you follow with the sauce! Let's get moving, boys!"

"For Christ's sake! Could you stop holding everyone up, Johnson? Chef Will looks like he's about to pass out! Get your act together!"

Li's forehead drooled sweat. The ladle trembled as he poured lamb jus onto perfectly roasted meat.

"NOW you decide to come back!" Aaron yelled. "What's the matter? Am I too mean? TOUGH CRAP! I want the chocolate soufflé for dessert, and it BETTER be standing when I get it!"

"He has some nerve demanding that after the hell he put me through! Go clear Table 50, Johnson! We'll set the cheese course shortly."

Li stumbled as he raced to the V.I.P. table, summoning all of his catlike reflexes to keep from falling on his face.

Paul seethed at the young waiter. "I can't believe you left those filthy plates on the table! You are ruining everything! But what else am I supposed to expect from a kid who couldn't finish college?"

Li winced. That one hurt. He just kept his head bent and cleared the table. Rosemary Hale watched him work, her eyebrows knitted together.

"Don't just throw the china into the sink, Johnson! I don't care how busy you are! Here's the cheese platter. The soufflé for Mr. Food Critic will be done soon."

"Hey! Food Boy! Where the hell is my dessert?"

PLEASE stop...I'm going to scream...

"Give me those plates, Johnson! I'll present the cheese! Tell Will to get the soufflés ready! I want them barely wiggling when they come out!"

"Here's the chocolate soufflé! The customer's lucky I didn't spit in it!"

Sweat drenched Li's hair. He held a tray with a delicate chocolate confection quivering in its ramekin.

Oh God...Please don't fall...Please please PLEASE...

Li's luck held. He set it on the Brents' table and bolted before another word was said.

"Where were you, Johnson? The soufflés for Table 50 are ready to go. If even one falls, I'll kill you. Get going!"

"FINALLY! I could have died and been reincarnated in the time it takes you to get here! Get the desserts on the table!"

With surgical care, the soufflés found their final resting places. Lips were licked around the table. Li quietly cleared the cheese plates.

"I just want you to know," Rosemary said, gently taking a hold of Li's elbow, "that the food is delicious, and you have been a wonderful server. Don't let them run over you."

He smiled at her, but it felt like she forced him to smile at knifepoint.

"Thank you, Mrs. Hale," he replied.

Turning to take the dirty dishes away, Li collided with Paul. A huge uproar of shattering china, falling silverware, and startled shouts destroyed the dinnertime peace. Blobs of leftover food soiled the carpet and splashed upon Paul's precious shoes.

A vein pulsed at the maître d's temple. His face swelled purple. He wheezed heavily.

"I...you...how...I...!"

Li's body drained of all color. He bustled about, trying to collect the debris. Paul's fingers stretched and curled like hungry snakes. His dark eyes drilled into the waiter's face.

"You are DEAD, Johnson!" he snarled under his breath. "Solo dish duty for the rest of this trip! You'll be grateful if I let you in this room again! Now get the hell away from me!"

Li fled for his life.

Stupid Paul...Stupid Will...Stupid, stupid, stupid ship...

Li scrubbed a saucepan, ignoring the screams of his elbows and knuckles. The mound of used dishes swayed like a cobra before him. His only battlement for defense was the tiny pile of clean flatware to his right. He sniffed heavily and little red lines rimmed his eyes.

"I heard it got pretty ugly tonight at dinner," a voice said from the double doors. Li wheeled around.

"What are you doing here, Travis?" Li asked, wiping his eyes with his sleeve.

"I had Anita cover for me while I checked on my friend. How are you holding up?"

"I don't want to talk about it." Li scoured the silver tureen.

"Uh huh...I'll believe that." He grabbed Li's shoulders and looked him dead in the eyes. Li dropped his gaze to the floor. "How long have you been crying?"

Li pulled away. "I don't cry. I haven't cried since my dad was in the hospital."

"You came pretty damn close tonight. I can tell. Why don't you quit?"

"I'm not a quitter."

"But you've been thinking about it?"

Li nearly scratched the tureen with the scrub brush. "How did you find out about tonight?"

"How else? A big, loud buzzard told me. I swear Mr. Brent could drink Scotch from a hose. And when he gets plastered, he lets everyone know how stupid they are. You were his favorite target."

"Gee, I feel so wonderful."

"Sarcasm noted. Plus, Paulie the Perfect came in after service and downed two shots of tequila, complaining about how you ruined the night. What exactly happened?"

Li mumbled.

"Speak up, Li. I left my ear trumpet in the last century."

"I dropped food on his shoes."

Travis suppressed a snort of laughter. "When I said give 'em hell, Liam, I didn't mean take the kamikaze route. You should be dead now. How Paulie let you live is a secret you'll have to spill, boy."

"It was an accident!"

"Hey...calm down...I'm on your side, remember? Honestly, I'm cheering that you pulled that off, accident or not." Travis picked up a rag and scrubbed a plate. "Charlegne must have saved you."

"What do you mean?"

"Are you really that blind? Paulie would lick the floor for Charlegne Jackson. He wouldn't do anything to look bad in front of her. That includes murdering the one waiter he hates more than all the others."

"Does he really hate me?"

"Have you suffered from head trauma recently? Paulie loathes the ground you walk on. I don't want to make you panic, but he told me he's out to get you fired."

"Maybe I should let him..."

"I thought you weren't a quitter?"

"I'm not. But if he fires me, I can get off this ship for good."

"But then who will give me free food?"

"I never gave you free food."

"Maybe you should start, so you'll feel guilty about leaving."

Li couldn't suppress a smile. "You know you shouldn't be helping me. Paul might show up and stab me with those unused champagne flutes."

"If he does, I'll have no shame doing my tequila trick." He handed the rag to his friend. "Actually, I have to get going. Anita is fending off catcalls by herself, and she needs a big strong man to protect her."

"When she finds one, try not to step on his toes, Travis."

"Har dee har. Look who developed a sense of humor all of a sudden." He gave Li a cheeky salute. "By the way, Her Royal Highness is sitting in the dining room alone. I thought you should be the one who tells her to clear out, seeing how she likes you."

"Why not Paul?"

"Would you want him there in the state he's in? Paulie's trying to find a way to get drunk without security catching on. He's in no condition to deal with people."

Travis left the kitchen.

Li unloaded a sigh, wiped his hands on the dishcloth, and pushed his way into the dining room. Paul had dimmed the lights, and the huge windows on the opposite end of the room framed a black sea. Li strode across the room, catching sight of a woman seated at a table near the entrance.

"Miss Jackson?"

She did not turn. A small lamp on the table cast an amber glow over her figure. Liquid silver pooled around her body. Her stiletto heels, cast off after dinner, lay tangled under her chair. Charlegne Jackson took a small sip from the glass of Rosé in her hand.

"Hello, Liam," she said. Her voice rose from the deepest part of her throat.

Li stopped short. "You...You know my name?"

"Jean Paul told me. Stupid little man, isn't he?"

Li didn't reply.

"I suppose you want to keep quiet so you don't lose your job. Thankfully, I don't have to worry about that." She knocked back the rest of the drink, pink champagne slipping like a thief down her throat. "Well, go on! What do you want to tell me?"

"Th-The dining room is closed, Miss Jackson."

"I'm aware of that. That's why I'm here." She poured out more Dom and began freeing her hair from the chignon she wore. "You're very ordinary-looking, you know?"

"A-Am I?"

"Such a stupid question. Life is full of stupid questions. Do you have any idea why I asked you to serve my table?"

"Was there a special reason?"

"Questions, questions, questions!" She plunked her glass down on the table. "Do I look like a woman who cares about answering everyone's questions?"

"I-I-I'm sorry—"

"Oh, shut up, Liam! I can't stand empty apologies. I'll tell you why I chose you. During my whole career, I've been surrounded by faces. They won't leave me alone. For once, I wanted to be served by someone who had a face I wouldn't remember. Then I saw you. You were perfect. I will never remember what you look like. Your face is totally forgettable."

Li shuffled his feet, but said nothing.

"It must be boring to look so average," Charlegne continued. She breathed in the aroma of her champagne. Her eyelids fluttered. "I don't think I've ever known what it's like to be average."

"But you wish you did?"

She turned to him abruptly. Her eyes narrowed into suspicious slits. "Why do you say that?"

Li swallowed. "It just slipped out."

Charlegne tried to divine the secrets of her future in the window. She fiddled with a tiny ring on her left hand.

"Have you ever thought about death, Liam?"

Li rocked on his feet. "Death, Miss Jackson?"

"Ah, so you have thought about it. I thought so. Who died?"

"Miss Jackson, I—"

"Who died, Liam?"

Li's baby blues traced the swirling pattern of the carpet. "My dad. Leukemia."

"Have you ever thought about dying yourself?"

Li's nervous bobbing got worse. "NO!"

Charlegne drew her fingernail along the mouth of her glass. It made a soft squeal like a distant whistle. "Death is seen as horrible, isn't it? Everyone tells me that it's the worst thing that can happen. But is it? Is it really the *worst* thing? I wonder…Would I be afraid to die? Would it be… Would it be wrong to say I want to die?" She downed her champagne again. "That is, of course, if you are allowed to live."

Li shivered. Charlegne shrieked with laughter.

"Just think!" she chimed, "You can wake up tomorrow and see your dear old Daddy again!"

CHAPTER 5

Room Service

Travis finished washing the used glassware in the bar sink at Temptations. He glanced at his friend bent over scratch paper scrawling numbers. Li, the only student in his cobbled-together poor man's university, was doing his self-administered "homework" again.

"Dude...It's after midnight," Travis said, "and you have breakfast service. It's okay to get some sleep."

Li looked up from the careworn workbook sprawled on the bar top before him. His pencil drummed rapidly against the pages. "I didn't have a chance to finish my equations before work started, Travis."

"Finish them later. Your eyelids are sagging."

"I don't want to fall behind."

"Li, you found those workbooks in a dumpster."

"Not in a dumpster!" His face flushed pink. "They were fifty cents each at the library in Long Beach." He added: "I found the economics textbook in the dumpster."

"You're an odd duck, Li." Travis sighed and unlocked the liquor cabinet. "So did you kick Ms. High-and-Mighty out of the dining room?"

Li scribbled radicals across the page. "Not after she asked me about dying. I went back and tackled the dishes."

"So she's just sitting there toasting suicide, eh?" He pulled out a bottle of gin and raised it in a mock toast. "To death, Charlegne! Hopefully it doesn't hurt much."

"I can't believe you just said that."

"Hey...It's no skin off my nose if she's thinking of offing herself. Besides, what would it hurt if the world loses one person, particularly one as self-entitled as Charlegne Jackson?"

Li's smoky blue eyes fumed. "You've never lost someone, have you?"

Travis thumped the bottle he was putting away onto the counter. "Oh God, Li. Don't go off on your damn father again."

Li slammed shut his workbook and slid off the barstool. "You know what...Maybe I will go to bed. I certainly don't want to upset you by talking about my dad."

Travis seized his friend's wrist. "Oh, okay...I'm sorry if I upset you. There. All better?"

A frown pinched Li's mouth. "All I'm saying is that losing one person affects many people. Yeah, I know. I talk too much about my father. But, when he died, my family lost more than financial security. My mom lost the man who hitchhiked across the country to attend her college graduation. My sister and I used to play Knights and Castles with him for hours until we got too big for the cardboard castle he built us. Dad was *taken* from us." Li dropped his eyes to his workbook, and the radicals began to look like little houses. "Every day I work my butt off to be a better son for him."

"Even though he's dead?

"He's still my dad, dead or alive."

Li sat down again and pored over his sums.

"Sometimes, Li, you drive me up the damn—"

"Shut up, Sally! I'm feeling fine! I don't need to go to bed!"

Aaron Brent kicked up a new rage outside Temptations, his voice shredding the midnight hush.

"Aw damn," said Travis. "I thought I got rid of him."

"We should make sure everything's okay. If he's as drunk as you painted him, things will get ugly."

"Somehow, risking my life wasn't on my itinerary tonight, but if you insist..."

Travis and Li left the lounge and watched Aaron sway as he stormed toward them. His bullfrog face bulged with blood, and he occasionally stopped to support himself on a wall. Sally Brent crept after him.

"You there!" The drunken man wagged a fat finger at Travis. "Bar Jockey! Get me a double Scotch on the rocks! Nah...Screw the rocks! Get it to me straight from the bottle!" He wobbled on his feet.

"I cut you off hours ago, Mr. Brent."

"Ha ha! You're a lousy comedian! Get my drink or I'll sue your ass!"

"I'm sorry, but we do have rules."

"I can get you some coffee," Li offered.

Aaron rounded on him. "Shut up, Food Boy! I don't need coffee, dammit!" He swung his arms wildly, grazing the wall with his knuckles. He turned around, as if deciding to seek service elsewhere, and collided with his wife.

"Christ, woman! Do you have to follow so close behind me? You're like a damn cat, creeping about on your toes!"

Sally crumpled with apologies. "I'm sorry, Aaron...I was distracted...I wasn't thinking where I was going...It was an accident...I'm sorry...."

"You damn well don't think! Someone ought to smack some sense in you, woman!"

"Aaron, honey..."

"SHUT UP!"

His hand made sharp, dry contact with Sally's cheek. It sounded like a whip crack. Sally stumbled backwards, her hip clanging against the glass railing surrounding the Atrium, an ugly red handprint branding her pale face. Her soft blue eyes drowned in tears.

Li strode forward, face alive with fury, but Travis pulled him back. "Don't do something stupid, Li. Get security."

"YOU ASSHOLE!"

Li's heart jumped to his throat. Charlegne was there, seething with rage. The Ice Queen had melted. The woman framed in the dining room doorway breathed energy and life. She was passionate and vicious. You could feel the blood burning through her body. A hot blush filled Li's face and neck. He could hardly believe this was the same woman.

Charlegne stormed to the couple, her loose, blond hair whipping behind her. Her chest and neck flushed red and heaved with every word she barked. Her voice could cut diamonds. "You disgusting beast! How dare you hit her! How DARE you lay your hands on her, you son of a bitch!"

"Lay off, lady!" Aaron retorted. "This has nothing to do with you!"

"The hell it doesn't! You just decide to hit your wife or whoever she is in front of me! If you lay your hands on her like that one more time, I'll do more than just notify the captain!" She turned to address Sally, who shrank away with huge teardrops dangling off her lashes. Charlegne's tone softened. "Come on, dear. You need some coffee."

She moved to take the woman gently by the arm, but the husband grabbed Charlegne's wrist with a shaking hand.

"I'm not letting my wife go with someone like you, Barbie!"

Charlegne whirled around, wrenched her arm from his grip, and slapped him hard across his swollen face. Aaron staggered back, blood-shot eyes wide with alarm, a booze-bloated parody of his wife earlier. Fury quickly supplanted the shock.

Charlegne stepped toward him, her voice calm, cold, firm. It was the deadliest sound Li had heard yet. Like a razor-sharp icicle inching towards a beating heart. "NEVER touch me like that again. I'll see you ROT in jail if you lay a hand on any woman. Mark. My. Words."

She took Sally by the elbow and led the woman away. The air seemed to freeze when she turned her back to him. Aaron's face darkened to a mottled purple. He pounded a fat fist into his open hand. It made a thick, meaty thump.

Li pulled away from Travis.

"Mr. Brent?" he said, struggling to keep his voice calm. He wanted no more incidents like this. "Let me get you a cup of coffee."

"I'll kill them," Aaron croaked. "I'll kill them both and shit on their corpses..."

He stumbled in the direction of the elevator.

Li needed help to walk to the crew's quarters. His feet had swollen until he could no longer tie his shoes. Travis, having secured the bar and lounge, supported his friend.

"That was one hell of a show," Travis said. "The Ice Princess extends a hand to a lowly serf. Talk about a change of heart. Or more like the purchase of one. I didn't know they sold working hearts at Saks."

Li seemed unfocused as they entered the elevator. "Did you notice anything peculiar about the situation?" he asked.

"Other than Charlegne showing genuine human concern? Not really. I pegged Aaron Brent as a wife beater from the first 'Dammit, Sally.'"

"There's something I'm supposed to remember about Sally Brent's face."

"I really don't remember it...except for the big bruise she'll have later."

Li winced from both the pain in his feet and the memory. "I've seen it somewhere before. OW! Don't make me lean on that foot!"

Travis corrected his stance. "Sorry, dude. You really took a pounding today, didn't you?"

Li chewed his lip. "It feels like my feet are broken."

"They might be. You'll need to take these shoes off. Hopefully you don't have a stress fracture."

Li redistributed his weight, grimacing as his foot touched the floor. "I'd hate to see Paul's face if I did have a broken foot."

"It would look like fury and ecstasy had sex on his face. Almost there, Li."

The elevator reached Deck Three, the dregs of the ship. They dismounted and hobbled down the passageway to the sleeping quarters.

"Why can't I get her face out of my head?" Li asked himself.

"A secret love that will become a borderline obsession?" Travis pushed open the door to the quarters with his hip. "The only thing I recall was that handprint."

"Something about her eyes..."

"Look, Li. You're stressed and exhausted. Take off those shoes, go to your bunk, and go to sleep. No self-assigned homework. Paulie will ride your ass hard tomorrow."

Li tried to stifle a yawn. "If he doesn't kill me first..."

"Charlegne will take care of that. You're her favorite now."

In the cabin, Li trundled to the restroom before going to his bunk and collapsing on the flimsy mattress. His feet throbbed. The man in the top bunk stirred.

"Yo, Li," he said. "Don't flop on the bunk. I'm trying to sleep."

"Sorry, David."

Li sat up, fiddled with his shoelaces, and began the painful exercise of removing his shoes. He gasped when the first one came off. After slipping off the second, he discarded his socks. Blisters speckled his red, swollen feet. His toes looked like dumpy thumbs.

"Oh Jesus, Li."

David, a deck attendant, crept down from the top bunk. Ever the officer, he looked ready for action, not a lock of his clipped, brown hair out of place. He switched on the overhead light and gazed down at his bunkmate's mutilated feet.

"What the hell did you do?" he asked. "Walk on broken glass?"

"I work for Paul McCaffrey."

"That'll do it." David extracted a needle and a rag from his belongings. "We need to lance those suckers before they get infected. Put your foot up."

Li did what he was told. David repeated his earlier question, and Li shared the story, all the way through to Charlegne rescuing Sally Brent.

"So she finally found a heart," David replied. "Let's hope the Wizard doesn't renege on the deal." He pricked a particularly nasty blister and washed Li's foot with the wet rag.

Li flinched. "Everyone says that she's some kind of heartless monster. I didn't get that impression at all."

"What impression did you get? Hold still." He uncapped a disinfectant spray.

"I'm not sure yet. She seems like a deeply unhappy woman. Her makeup was too perfect. YOW! You could have warned me it would sting!"

"I did. I told you to hold still. Hold this rag on your foot but don't wipe."

Li wrapped his foot. "Why do you have all this stuff?"

"Li, I've been working for the Howard Line for eleven years. You pick up a few things. I used to get nasty blisters too, but I learned quickly. Let me take a look." The rag fell. "Okay. Looks fine. Let's do the next one."

"I wonder why she was thinking about death."

"Who knows? I don't understand creative people. Come on, don't dawdle. Get your foot up here." Li did so, biting his lip until it threatened to bleed. David set to work. "You must have caught her in some weird creative state. Maybe she's designing a collection of funeral wear."

"I think she remembered something. She kept playing with this little ring."

David wiped another burst blister. "A ring?"

"Yeah...this tiny diamond one. Didn't look that expensive. Why would she have that?"

"Women like jewelry, Li."

"No, that can't be it. From what I saw, it looked almost worthless. Charlegne Jackson would own the most expensive jewels. This ring was out of character."

"I'm going to spray your foot now." The young waiter closed his eyes and bit his lip harder. David dispatched with the disinfectant. "There. All done."

Li opened his eyes. "Thanks a bunch. I feel loads better."

"I'm still worried about that swelling. You better get Doc Innsbrook to check it out." He picked up the cast-off dress shoes. "What's your shoe size anyway?"

"Ten-and-a-half."

"That's it then. These shoes are a size too small. Why do you have them?"

Li mumbled.

"Well THAT was certainly helpful. Speak up, kid."

"They were all I could afford. I got them at a thrift store. They didn't have my size so I had to make do."

"That explains those ratty old sneakers under your bed."

Li's eyes focused on his sore feet. "I can only afford one pair of shoes a year."

David stood and removed a perfectly shined pair of dress shoes from under the bunk. He handed them to Li.

"Take them. They're too big on me."

"No, I'll be fine. Really. I couldn't take them from you."

"I'm not letting you walk out tomorrow with shoes that'll hurt you. Take these or I'll force you to sleep in them."

Li hesitated, but then accepted the shoes. "Thanks. I really have nothing to give you in return. If there's anything I can—"

David raised a hand, cutting Li off. "Don't worry about it. We're bunk-mates. Just promise me that you won't rock the bed in the middle of the night."

"I promise."

"Good. Now get your butt in bed, kid."

The cabin door opened and Marisol, one of Li's fellow servers, walked in with her sharply-taloned hands on her hips.

"Sorry to wake you," she said, checking her reflection in her acrylics and not sounding sorry at all, "but there's a room service call. A cup of

Oolong tea to Verandah Deck 5. Charlegne Jackson. She asked specifically for you, Johnson." She pivoted on her heels and flounced away.

David turned to Li. "Do you want me to—?"

Li shook his head. "We both know that won't go over well. Hopefully it'll be quick. I'm going to steal your shoes for this."

"By all means. I'm going to bed. Try not to make too much noise when you return. We both have morning shifts tomorrow."

It took Li nearly fifteen minutes to get his new shoes on, limp to the elevator, head to the beverage station on the Verandah Deck, make the tea—*Of course, there wouldn't be any ready*—and carry it gingerly to the stateroom. His back popped as he set the tray down in the passageway. His knuckles rapped on the door. "Room service."

The door snapped open before he could turn to leave. Charlegne, dressed in nothing but a silk excuse for a bathrobe, stood there, soft, gray pouches under her eyes. Behind her, Steven Danforth lay on the bed, naked as he was on the day he was born.

CHAPTER 6

Breakfast

"That bastard! Is he hung-over or something? How can he say that my Hollandaise is too eggy? The sauce has egg yolks in it!"

Li tossed Mr. Brent's barely licked plate of crab cake eggs benedict onto the pass-through. Chef William flung the food into the trash and barked at his cooks for a third refire. Li, armed with a full carafe of coffee, swept out of the kitchen and returned to the Captain's Table.

"You seem much more relaxed this morning," said Rosemary Hale, accepting a fresh cup.

Li smiled, this time genuine. "I have new shoes today." He wiggled his toes in David's dress shoes.

Rosemary forked through her poached egg. "I haven't seen Charlegne this morning. Do you know where she is?"

"No, ma'am."

The stress lines around her lips softened. "Perhaps she's sick in her stateroom."

"We'll send a steward to check on her, if you wish, Mrs. Hale."

"Oh...no rush..."

"Food Boy!" Aaron screamed from across the room. "Where is my breakfast?"

"Duty calls, Mrs. Hale. I'll be back shortly." Li returned to the kitchen, retrieved the corrected breakfast plate, and rushed to the Brents' table. Aaron's face flushed scarlet and sweat percolated on his forehead. Sally had a large bruise stamped on her cheekbone.

"You take too long! What will it take to get some decent service on this godforsaken ship? Where's my food?"

Li placed the amended dish before his customer. "Will there be anything else, sir?"

"Where are the potatoes? A decent breakfast has potatoes!"

"The crab cake benedict doesn't come with potatoes, sir. It comes with grilled asparagus."

"Blech! Rabbit food! I want potatoes!"

"Might I suggest the bacon potato hash on the side?"

"Hmph! It'll have to do! But don't screw this up!" He began plowing through his crab cake.

Li turned to Sally. "And you, ma'am? Would you like anything else?" *Like a divorce attorney*, he added inwardly.

Sally flinched and directed the traffic of her scrambled eggs around her plate. "No...No, I'm fine."

Chef Will scowled at this new request. "Oh for the love of God! Didn't you tell him what came with the crab? You did? Then he's just being a bastard." He massaged his temple. "Luis! Fire a potato hash on the fly! And Johnson, answer the room service line. I hear it ringing."

Li hooked the receiver with his index finger and balanced it between his shoulder and his ear. "Room service. How may I help you?"

The woman on the other end snapped at him. "Quail egg amuse-bouche, whole wheat toast, and black coffee to be sent to Miss Jackson's stateroom. Verandah Deck 1."

"The amuse-bouche is reserved for the dining room and is only given at the chef's discretion."

The woman seemed to snarl at him. "Are you perfectly willing to risk your job and livelihood by defying Miss Jackson's direct orders? Do you need a reminder about who you are serving?"

Li felt a headache start to brew between his eyes. "Very well, ma'am. How would you like your egg cooked?"

"It's not MY food!"

"Very well. How would Miss Jackson like her egg?"

"Sunny side up. And make sure you send that Lenny boy or whoever he is." The other end clicked off.

Li couldn't see how anyone could survive on just a thimbleful of food. But it wasn't his job to reason whys or wherefores. "Sunny side up quail egg amuse and whole wheat toast for Cabin V1!" The chefs called back the order. Luis handed him the completed hash for Aaron Brent, which Li knew would be returned for something as stupid as the wrong color plate.

As he neared the table, a happy woman's voice funneled into his ears.

"She always looks like a cornered rabbit. I can't understand why she married that man. Do you suppose he was abused as a child and now takes it out on everyone else? Linda knew this man who was assaulted by a neighbor and ended up firing birdshot at passing teenagers. I hope that man isn't armed on this ship. That was a wonderful idea, Honeybunch, about asking her to join me on Catalina. She just needs a friend...and time away from her husband."

If that's Sally Brent, Li thought, *I'll drop food on Paul's shoes again.*

A man responded. "I knew you wouldn't want to be alone, my little cupcake."

And if that's Aaron Brent, I'll EAT Paul's shoes.

The Brents had abandoned the remnants of their food at the table. A new couple had replaced them. The woman's voice sped over her tongue at a velocity no formula could measure. Li tacked on his friendliest smile and hustled over to them.

"So sorry about that," he said, hastily bussing the table. "Allow me to offer our popular potato bacon hash as compensation."

"Oh, no problem!" Mrs. Piston Jaw replied, her ample lips spreading into a smile. "It's our fault really. We were chatting with this couple we met after dinner last night. The Brents. It's a shame they couldn't stay and join us, wasn't it Joshy-poo?"

"I'm afraid you'll have to excuse my wife," the man said. "She likes to share." He speared a potato cube on his fork and inspected it. "You don't give free food to ALL the passengers, do you?" His eyes shifted from potato to waiter.

"Actually, sir, we do."

The man glared at Li as if trying to melt the boy's organs with his mind.

Li felt his intestines twist into nervous knots. "Erm...are you ready to order, sir?"

The customer popped the scrutinized morsel into his mouth. "A man has to wonder, you know. Wouldn't want him to think you were being too friendly with his wife."

39

"Oh Josh!" the woman said, "don't tease me!" She giggled. Li drew up the fantasy of her as a Southern belle, blushing and twittering behind her grandmother's fan.

"I wouldn't dream of it, Daphne," He lowered his lips onto the back of her hand and pecked it. However, his eyes continued to burrow into Li's soul like twin augers.

Trying to ignore the look of hate and disgust, Li proceeded to advise them on the menu, took their orders, listened as briefly as he could to Daphne's compliments, and went back to the kitchen. The couple's voices shadowed him.

"Isn't he sweet, Joshy? Complimentary food and attentive service. This potato hash is just delicious!"

"He's practically a baby, Daphne dear. Don't make him chase after you."

"I don't know what you're talking about, Honeybunch."

"The hell you don't. If I even catch him sniffing at your skirt—"

The swinging kitchen doors clipped the tail-end of their conversation.

"Paul's fuming that you're taking the breakfast order to Her Majesty," Chef Will said upon Li's return. "Then again, he's been out to get you all morning. Did you know I caught him trying to sprinkle habanero chili onto one of your breakfast plates? If I were you, I'd give him a wide berth. Here's Charlegne's breakfast. We'll keep an eye on your tables while you deliver it. Now get your butt moving, Johnson!"

Li sped to the service elevator in the back of the kitchen, pushing the room service cart topped with a cloche-covered dish. As he strode out onto the Verandah Deck, he swerved to avoid hitting David.

"Whoa! Watch your step, Li! I guess my shoes are working wonders for you. What do you have there anyway?"

"Charlegne's breakfast. Sorry, I can't stay and chat. I have a table in the dining room waiting on me."

"Try not to run anyone else down."

Li brushed past his bunkmate and arrived at V1, Charlegne's stateroom. He performed his standard duties: placed the tray outside the cabin door, knocked, announced "Room Service," and walked away. This time Charlegne did not answer. Li left without being seen.

The thought struck him as he trundled into the service elevator again. *Last night, I delivered tea to her in V5. Now it seems her stateroom is V1. Then whose cabin was she in last night?*

CHAPTER 7

The Ice Queen

She stepped out of the pool and strode toward him, her long, blond hair slung over one shoulder in a loose cascade of wet curls. She did not wear makeup, but her eyelashes were thick and dark as if combed with fresh mascara. Her lips, naturally pink, parted with a sigh. The man watched a single bead of moisture drip off her wet hair and trace a path down the curve of her neck, over the landscape of her collar bones, and into the nook of her cleavage.

It was a cousin to the beads of sweat following the line of his jaw.

She's ruining my marriage.

A seagull squawked overhead, jerking Martin Hale out of his Charlegne Jackson daydream, scattering the drips of sweat gathered in the cleft of his chin. He daubed away the newcomers brewing along his hairline. His knuckles, clenched around the arm of his deck chair, were white as bone.

I hate this bitch.

The chill of the sea breeze helped. Martin turned his face toward the wind and ocean spray. Catalina Island lay just a few miles beyond the ship, rising out of the waves with the superiority of an old sea god. And his mind conjured Charlegne from the sea mist.

Charlegne! Millions of boys across the globe cited her as their first: the first fantasy girl, the first orgasm, the first wet dream. She had graced the covers of every fashion magazine on Earth. You couldn't walk past a newsstand without seeing her staring back at you. And for gentlemen with a little imagination, Charlegne's "for-the-camera-only" bedroom eyes hypnotized them into complete submission.

Not a single man on the planet could explain why she fascinated him.

She never did nudes. Her swimsuits were always one-piece. There were no exaggerations in her figure. She was slim and healthy, but with feminine lines and curves. She never posed in bizarre angles or shapes like the fashion mavens adored. There was hardly anything provocative about her modeling. It was just...the way she existed. She stood differently than other women. She moved differently. She occupied space in a way that most people couldn't help but gravitate toward.

The woman is a witch, plain and simple.

Yes, Charlegne was a damn witch. There was restraint—modesty, really—in her appearance. People saw glamor, ice and diamonds, a woman drowning in champagne and Swarovski. This was not Charlegne. She was in control. She would slam the door on any suggestive behavior. She played it cool. Somehow, this made all the little monsters found in men tear at themselves with dirty screams.

Her eyes did most of the work. Martin remembered the way they seemed to burn through you. Like lasers. A woman who could incinerate your soul with her gaze, was capable of violent, passionate feeling. It boiled beneath her skin. You couldn't model like that, express yourself with that sort of laser intensity, without being capable of suffering. Though, in later years dubbed "The Ice Queen," Martin knew Charlegne could feel intense emotion, so intense that it would destroy a weaker soul.

Her eyes said it all. To him, they said one thing loud and clear.

You can never have me.

Martin did not love Charlegne, not like he loved Rosemary. But he wanted her in the filthiest way his body could imagine.

"Sir?"

For the second time, Martin wrenched himself from his fantasy. His right hand hovered above his waistband.

"Sir, is there anything I can help you with?"

The deck attendant lingered at Martin's elbow.

"Oh...uh. No, I think I'm fine." He hauled himself into an upright position, stretching out the cramps in his fingers. "Just...uh...waiting for the boats to get their act together, so we can go to the island. How much longer anyway?"

"About fifteen minutes, sir. The tenders are scheduled to depart at ten."

"Good. I...uh...I have to wait for my wife. We won't miss them, will we?"

"Oh no, sir. The boats run every ten minutes."

"Well, that's a huge relief. I—"

"Oh dear. I'm too early. It figures. I'm always too early for things. Then again, we did just make these plans, and Josh had to leave breakfast sooner than he intended."

Martin heard the woman long before he saw her. Lost under a hurricane of black hair, she scrambled up from the lower decks. Her lips never stopped moving.

The attendant approached her. "Ma'am? Is there anything I can help you with?"

She shoved back a mess of hair. "Oh! I'm sorry. I didn't realize there was anyone up here. Is this the Seaview Deck? I'm supposed to meet someone up here. At least, I think it was here. It could have been the Lido Deck."

"The Seaview Deck is just behind you, ma'am, but perhaps you'd care to wait over by the pool instead? I'll take you to the port side closest to the Sunbathing Deck, so you can get the most sun. After all, the shade of the Seaview Deck is very cold in the morning."

"Oh, nothing is too cold for me. I used to spend Christmas in Minnesota. Now that's some serious cold weather. I remember when the pipes froze while my grandfather took a shower—"

"You'd probably enjoy waiting for your friend in the sunshine."

She wrestled the tentacles of her hair into a ponytail. "Oh, she's not my friend, really. I only met her at breakfast. Poor woman. Completely trapped under her husband's thumb. The way he bullies her. But enough about that. I'm sure poor Sally wouldn't want me to gab on about her marriage. I do feel bad for her, though. She's just so...meek."

The attendant pulled out the chair next to Hale, who opened his mouth in protest and decided against it. "It's a shame, ma'am. Could I get you anything else?"

"Oh, I don't know. I really shouldn't. Breakfast was just delicious. And our waiter was so cute. Quite young, too. The most ADORABLE blue-gray eyes. Oh, what the heck! It IS my vacation. I'd like an iced tea with lemon, please."

"Right away, ma'am."

The woman turned to Martin, who was slumped in his chair. "This cruise is just fabulous! I haven't been on many, you know, but the few I did go on were mostly for families. It's so pampered here. I feel like a queen! The staff here takes such good care of us, like...like shepherds with their flock."

Martin rolled his eyes and sank his chin to his chest.

"It was really nice of Josh's sister to give us this surprise cruise. We really did need to get away for a while."

I think I need to get away for a while, Martin thought.

"Of course, Marcia warned me about stewards who help themselves to a little easy money and captains who are too friendly with their passengers, but I think she was just jealous. The Howard Line is perfect. I couldn't find fault if I tried!"

They certainly don't discriminate against passengers.

"And the weather has just been—Oh my God! It's HER!"

Martin felt his little monster moan. The shielded, golden head of Charlegne Jackson, in rich, sensitive flesh, rose from the starboard-side ladder. He let a small grunt escape his lips. She wore a white, one-piece bathing suit with side cutouts revealing the tight cinch of her waist. A wide-brimmed purple sunhat guarded her face from the sunlight. Martin watched several locks of her hair tickle the pearly skin of her breast, sometimes slipping quietly underneath her swimsuit. His hand twitched. It became uncomfortable to sit upright.

If Rosie knew how I felt, she would kill me. She might know already. God help me if she does. She just keeps me around because I belong to her. The only way she can survive this...problem...is if I belong to her. God, this hurts.

The woman's relentless commentary droned on next to him.

"She's so untouched. It's like turning the pages of *Vogue* all over again. Don't you find it incredible how some people never seem to age? They have all the luck, don't they? And just imagine being Charlegne for a day...the clothes...the jewelry...the trips around the world..."

That's all they ever see. The diamonds...the champagne...the smooth elegance of each ivory limb. Oh hell, I'm going to burst.

Charlegne, overhearing this flood of praise, raised her hand in acknowledgment. Martin traced the languid curl of her fingers, and the moisture evaporated from his throat. From his poolside vantage point, he watched her amble onto the neighboring Sunbathing Deck, deposit herself onto a lounge chair, snap her fingers, and give orders to the attendant. He saw the way her pink lips shaped the words. She turned to him then. Those lips parted into a sleepy smile, revealing the clean, white pattern of her teeth. Sunshine stroked the curve of her cheek with golden fingers.

Even the gods love her.

"And I'll always remember that *Vogue* spread fifteen years ago. Maybe I could have her sign a copy for me. I always bring an issue of *Vogue* on trips. I don't suppose you know what I'm talking about. Men aren't concerned with fashion. My husband didn't even react when I said I saw Charlegne in the dining room, last night. He just sat there like a big mannequin. Well, no matter. I remember she wore this long white gown by Christian Lacroix, I think. Unbelievably couture. It's funny, though, it always reminded me of a wedding dress."

The closest thing she ever came to wearing a wedding gown.

Charlegne lathered her limbs with sunscreen. Martin felt the top of his inseam grow stiff. He rested his hand there and hoped he didn't start sweating. Charlegne took extra care to smooth out the lotion on her legs, leaving her skin gleaming gold in the strengthening sunlight. The deck attendant deposited a steaming cup of coffee on the table to her right.

She's the most beautiful bitch in the world.

Again the sleepy smile, the hat tilted to keep the sun from melting the ice blue of her eyes, the swelling atom of sweat coursing down Martin's jawline.

"*Oh no!*"

Martin yelped at the woman's outburst. He wiped away the sweat on his hairline again. His heart moved into his throat.

"How could I be so stupid? I was supposed to meet Sally on the Seaview Deck at ten! I hope she hasn't left the ship yet. I don't want her to think I totally forgot about her. What with everything she has to endure." She ran her hand underneath the lounge chair. "Oh, this is not my morning. I left my purse in my cabin. I'll have to go down to the stateroom, grab my bag and the magazine, and come back here to meet Sally. I hope she won't mind it if we get Charlegne's autograph. I don't think she would. Lord, if I stay here talking your ear off, I'll never get off this ship! Sorry to run, Mr.—Oh, I never learned your name. Nice talking to you!"

She bustled down the starboard-side ladder, continuing to make all her private concerns public.

Martin exhaled. *Oh thank sweet baby Jesus, she's gone!* He stole a glance at the sunbathing figure to his left. Charlegne, sunhat sheltering her face, dozed like a cat, letting the sunshine envelop her. Martin's little monster whined.

I hate her. I hate her because she makes it hurt.

He moved towards the starboard-side ladder. The sea breeze didn't help him as much as he thought it would.

Dustin, how could you?

Rosemary felt the wind take a fancy to her hair. Standing at a strip of observation deck at the extreme tip of the bow, nicknamed the Prow Deck, she tried to settle her heartbeat. She suddenly felt like Kate Winslet in *Titanic*, embraced by the breeze, unaware of disaster. *Where the hell is my Leo?* The crinkle of paper shifting in the wind brought her eyes down to her hands.

She clutched a folded sheet of paper. Her knuckles burned red while the rest of her fingers glowed white. Her green eyes darkened to nearly black.

This is all wrong. She should be the body floating in the river.

Her fingernails punctured the skin of the letter. A muscle tensed along her throat. Rosemary unfolded the note, and her eyes swallowed the first line. Her pupils started to tighten into snake-like slits.

Rosie,
I know you love me, and I also know you won't understand this, but—

She stopped. There was a sharp, stabbing pain just to the left of her heart. She drew in a large gulp of salty air through her nose, trying to squeeze the knife out of her chest. Her pupils relaxed.

No, Dustin. I don't understand.

She wanted to hurt. Yes, she wanted to hurt someone badly. She wanted to make that someone suffer.

A distraction. That's all it is. I need something to distract me from this javelin in my heart. Isn't that how bullies work? How did that get in my head?

Rosemary wrapped her fingers around the railing and leveled her gaze with the far horizon. The sky and sea were perfect mirrors of each other. This cruise should have been peaceful. After a depressing visit to the doctor, Rosemary needed a vacation. Then she saw Charlegne, white and golden, the perfect princess of the land of milk and honey, glide past her before the ship even thought about departing. And then there was the look in Martin's eyes—the slight dilation of his pupils.

I came so close. It was like Fashion Week all over again. I was back in the tent I shared with that bitch. She sailed in, trailed by that mob of nitwits, their tongues wagging out of their mouths. The hate was there. The same old hate as always. I saw her push Dustin over the edge again. But I thought I could handle it this time. Focus on the clothes. Focus on the collection. Then I looked at Marty's face...his eyes...the way his pupils dilated just a little. I knew it then! I knew he loved her! Oh Marty, you son of a BITCH!

Her fingers squeezed the handrail like they would around someone's neck.

It was insanity. I have no other defense for it. Everything just started to go dark...like passing into a tunnel. All I could focus on was Charlegne's neck, white and smooth and untouched. She laughed then, I think. One of those patronizing little titters she likes to give. The muscles along her throat bobbed up and down and up and down. I thought, "It would be so easy to stop that bobbing." And my hands...I don't remember moving them...they were pressed against those muscles. I felt them shift and pull under my fingers. I pushed. The only way to stop a pull is with a push. Simple physics. The muscles trembled. I think there was a shout then. I pushed harder. Then more shouts. There was a big burst of light, like a sun exploding. I remember the relief! Even as my fingers cramped, I remember how all my other muscles relaxed. Like the muscles in my heart. And didn't Charlegne relax too? She gave this weird little sigh. The lines around her mouth started to smooth out. I think she even smiled.

"Attention passengers. The tenders to Catalina Island are departing now. Please proceed to Deck Three. Thank you for sailing on the Howard Line."

Rosemary pulled her thoughts from the wet fog of her memories. She used the heel of her palm to mush away the unexpected tears. She turned toward the Sunbathing Deck, her eyes outlining the hard ridges of the island looming just beyond the ship. *Go back to your cabin, meet Marty, and go to the island. You know she won't leave the ship today. There's no risk that she and Marty will see each other. No danger. Put on your happy face, Rosie.*

She tortured her lips into a smile. She drew her gaze away from the island and back onto the ship. A golden halo of hair rose from the ladder in front of her.

CHARLEGNE!

Rosemary knew it was her, knew it in that deep place where intuition becomes knowledge. Somewhere in her brain, there was a distant boom like faraway thunder. She wheeled around, strangling the railing with her hands while she tried to stifle the balloon of rage inflating in her chest. She could not, could not, could NOT deal with that woman right now! The salt in the sea mist bit her skin. The letter trapped under her fingers felt white-hot.

If I stay here, she'll mention Dustin. If she does, I'll kill her.

She marched to the Seaview Deck, trying to put as much distance between her and the bitch as she could. Her eyes bulged with new tears.

CHAPTER 8

Scandal

"Are you going on the Catalina crew excursion, Li? They plan to go to the Airport-in-the-Sky and eat enough buffalo to repopulate the prairie. Got to be much more interesting than doling out Chef Will's 'boof burger-nine.'"

"*Boeuf bourguignon*," Li corrected. "It's a beef stew in red wine with—"

"Earth to Li!" Travis knocked hard on Li's skull. "You're off the clock. Get out of waiter mode and get moving. You're holding up the mess line."

Li spooned scrambled eggs onto his plate. "Sorry, Travis. Spending all day explaining dishes to people sort of gets stuck in my mind."

"Is there any way for you to refrain from thinking while we get our breakfast? Carlos is saying some pretty colorful Spanish obscenities behind me."

Li shifted down the buffet line. He heard someone behind him exhale an expression of annoyance in some Scandinavian tongue. "Are you going on the excursion, Travis?"

Travis ladled a sea of gravy onto two and a half biscuits. "You bet. I hate staying cooped up on the ship. Any excuse to get off is welcome. I could use a buddy."

"I'd like that, but—"

"Hurry up, will you? I'm starving down here!" The new voice swore with a French accent.

Travis stacked a tower of bacon onto his plate. "Let's get a seat before we're mugged."

"Do you really need that much bacon, Travis?"

"We made a rule. No discussing my eating habits. I don't make fun of all that fruit you eat. Trust me...I have a few gems in my head."

"Doc Innsbrook must love seeing this."

"Li, I have to deal with drunk rich people. I should be allowed to eat what I want." He shoved a fat forkful of gravy-drenched biscuit into his mouth, making his cheeks bulge. "You never answered my question, Li."

"I was going to say—"

"Johnson!" shouted an all-too familiar, all-too irritating voice. "We have business we need to discuss!"

"—that I never get a word in edgewise."

Paul stormed through the aisles dividing the cafeteria tables. Heads swiveled on their necks to follow him.

"You have a shit ton of explaining to do, Johnson!" Paul yelled across the room.

"Gee, that's a surprise," Travis said. "Next he'll tell you that you are a waiter in the dining room. The man misses nothing."

"Paul, if this about your shoes—" Li began.

"If you don't want my foot in your ass, Johnson, I'd suggest you keep THAT little apology to yourself. Now what the hell is this about you and Charlegne last night?"

A few heads bobbed above the rest like curious flamingos.

"I delivered her tea."

"HA! I've heard many euphemisms, but 'delivering tea' has to be the worst one yet!"

"Excuse me?"

"What time was this so-called delivery?"

"What does that have to do with anything?"

"So you won't answer the question?" Paul barked over his shoulder. "Told you, Jasper! The kid's a slippery little twerp!"

Travis waved his loaded fork at Paul, gravy slopping onto the tabletop. "If you spent less time being a prick, Paulie, maybe we could get to the point of this interrogation."

"Shove it, Patrelli! And don't call me Paulie! Jasper saw Mr. Popular here go to Charlegne's room. She stood in the doorway wearing nothing but a bathrobe. A SILK bathrobe. She was expecting you, wasn't she?"

"He told you, Paulie. He delivered tea to her. That's kind of his job. Leave him alone."

"Patrelli, I would have to be drunk out of my skull to want to talk to you. Go shove a bagel down your throat."

"And why was Jasper spying on Her Royal Highness, anyway?"

Paul waved off the insinuation. "He worked as the night shift attendant. Forget about him. The real news is he heard the loudest sex noises coming from the room not long after Johnson was there!" Several men whooped and applauded, jeering in at least a dozen languages. "Jasper said it sounded like someone rode the mattress like a mechanical bull."

"I didn't do anything!" Li shouted.

"Don't yell, Johnson! No wonder she had a preoccupation with you. I couldn't understand why she wanted YOU to serve her. Nobody wants you."

"David can vouch for me! I went to bed not long after I left!"

"You're going to hang your hopes on that?"

"What do you mean?"

"You mean you don't know?" A slimy grin outlined Paul's lips. Li drew up the image of a hungry snake. "David said he saw you leave, but doesn't know when you returned. You were gone for a while he thought."

"I-I swear I—"

"Why else would you be in her room?"

"But it wasn't her room!"

Li's hands rocketed to his mouth, and the color of his face matched the Oxnard strawberries he had been eating. The crowd in the mess hall settled. This new silence pressed tightly against Li's ears.

Paul's voice stayed calm. "Why do you say that, Johnson?"

Li shook his head wildly back and forth.

"Were you in her room or not?"

Li repeated the action.

The hungry snake grin widened. "Sex with a passenger while on duty. You know that's a violation of ship policy."

Travis intervened. "Okay, okay. Let's break this up. Paulie, you don't have any proof. And neither does Jasper. Li didn't do anything. Let's just eat our breakfast and get out of here." He tucked into his palace of bacon like he hadn't eaten in days.

The room seemed to retract into a caricature of a normal breakfast. Li felt every eye crawling on the back of his neck. He returned to his plate and poked a cantaloupe wedge with his fork. His heart drooped around his knees. "It was better when people ignored me. When did this turn into high school?"

Travis slowed his eating. "Why didn't you tell me about Charlegne?"

"Travis, I—"

"I mean...I had to wonder why she was so keen on you. That whole 'I will never remember what you look like' thing never really felt right."

"Travis, I swear I didn't—"

"Sorry for saying this, but a guy has issues when his friend sleeps with his former fantasy girl."

"I did not sleep with her!"

Travis set his loaded fork on the plate, propped his elbows on the table, and folded his hands. He stared Li down like a judge appraising the damned. "Then how do you know that the room wasn't hers?"

Li told him.

Travis relaxed his pose. "So it's the old room service gag, eh? I can't believe that you'd actually be that observant at one o'clock in the morning."

"Well, I was! Charlegne wasn't in her room last night, but she was for breakfast!"

"A fact that only YOU know!"

"I'm telling you the truth, Travis!"

"You should have stuck to sleeping with the purser like Carlos does."

"Why don't you believe me?"

Travis picked at the bacon with his fingers. "You know you totally threw your neck into a noose, Li. Paulie will see you hanged for this. Hell, he'd hold the rope. Good-bye cushy cruise job."

"I didn't do anything! What will it take to get you to believe me?"

"Who knows? Maybe you can have Charlegne make a public appearance. Really ham it up with the tear-stained hankie, a cup of Darjeeling, and a hearty cry of 'I did not have sexual relations with this what's-his-face!'"

Li's mouth tensed into a scowl. "That's not a bad idea."

"Wait...what?"

"Talking to Charlegne. If no one will listen to me telling the truth, they will definitely listen to her."

"Ha! Good luck with that! Once word gets out that you had a private chat with Madame Frostbite, you'll be marooned off the Ensenada harbor in a rowboat with a map to Mexico City. Hope your Spanish has gotten better."

"I'm not going to lose my job, Travis. I won't let them fire me without knowing the truth."

"You poor, innocent, idealistic child." He swished milk in his mouth, inflating his cheeks in a cartoonish parody of a chipmunk storing nuts.

"I guess I'm not going ashore with you then."

Travis choked. "Hey now! Why are you punishing me?"

"Who said anything about punishment?"

"What will you do? You know Charlegne will have a swarm of sycophants kissing her elegant behind. How do you plan to get through to her?"

"I'm sure there are ways."

"Not without security stalking you. If Charlegne doesn't want to be disturbed, Captain Crayle himself would throw anyone off the ship who so much as cast a shadow on her."

"If I can't talk to her, then I guess I'll have to find out who slept with her last night."

CHAPTER 9

Catalina Island

"Damn tourists! Get out of my way, stupid!"

The golf cart veered wide. Steven Danforth ducked out of the way just as the tire scraped the heel of his $300 Oxfords. The driver swore as he sped up the hills of Avalon. Several parents clamped their hands to their children's ears.

Incredible, Steven thought. *Even on a damn island in the middle of the damn ocean where people drive golf carts instead of cars, there's still road rage. People never change.*

"How awful! Are you okay, sir? I can't believe people can be so rude!"

A woman with a half-tamed ponytail of black hair descended upon Steven like a nurse on the battlefield.

"That man just came out of nowhere! Ducking and diving and swerving through the crowd like he was on the run. I can't imagine why he was in such a hurry! I'm surprised he didn't hurt anyone. That was a very close shave he gave you. Are you sure you're all right?"

"Oh...um...I think so. He just nicked my shoe."

"It was so rude of him to swear at you like that. Especially in front of all these kids. Just terrible. If I was lucky enough to be a mother, I would have DIED to know my children heard that sewer mouth. Absolutely filthy. Wouldn't you say so, girls?"

Steven's eyebrows launched up his forehead as he saw Priscilla Reilly stand beside the woman. "I thought I had seen the worst living in L.A. Some people just have no class, Daphne."

"Aren't you a little far from the ship, Priscilla?" Steven asked. "Charlegne can hardly blow her nose without you being there to hold the Kleenex."

Priscilla fussed with the drape of her dress, which drooped like sad woolen swags of Spanish moss. "She gave me the afternoon off. She told me so last night. I guess she just wanted some space. I gathered she had her fill of human interaction after last night. Don't you think so, Steven?"

"You always seem to know too much, Priscilla."

"The walls are thin. Remember that." She turned back to her travel companion. "I simply must take you to this little dress shop I heard so much about, Daphne! All custom pieces done in the most exquisite fabrics. We'll find something gorgeous for you to wear to dinner tonight. If we step up the pace a little, we can go there just before our tour of the Casino."

"Oh yes, Priscilla! Sounds wonderful! But remember, Sally asked us if we could stop at the drug store so she can get something for her headache."

"Oh yes, of course. We'll go after the dress shop. Confidentially, Daphne, I think Sally's husband is her only real headache."

The two women bustled back across the street to a woman whose face cowered behind a lifeless sheet of blond hair. She seemed to wilt into the scenery.

Could have been very pretty if she let herself think so, Steven thought. His eyes swung around to where the ship rested on the cushion of a Pacific horizon, a white diamond couched in blue satin. *She's no Charlegne Jackson.*

He pictured his boss lounging on the thin strip of beach just ahead of him, warming her fading tan and clad in white, her favorite color, the color of ice.

And virgin brides...Let's not forget that she almost got married. She certainly didn't forget. I think it's impossible for her to forget. She made sure her memories would last. She'll carry that copy of Vogue *with her until the day she dies.*

He drew up the picture of her in the Lacroix dress, white on ivory crowned with gold. His own little monster stretched and yawned. Grunting under his breath, Steven shoved the drowsy beast back into bed.

Goddamn woman. He unbuttoned the collar of his three-piece suit. *She's got her claws in my throat, all right. She'll drag me to Paris...Rome...then Sydney...and I wouldn't be able to refuse her! Worse, she knows it. She knows that I'd bend over backwards and kiss my own ass to do whatever she wanted. I hate that bitch. I hate the fact she makes me love her. She can pretend to care, just like she pretended last night. But when I saw her before dinner, I knew she hated the sight of me. Love disgusts her. She is incapable of loving anyone ever again. She just loves that I belong to her, that I'm her stupid little slave.* His eyes hardened on the ship. *Unless I ask questions. Charlegne hates them. Maybe I ought to ask more questions about that little wimp who—* He checked his watch. *Dammit. Eleven o'clock already? I'm going to be late for that damn tour.*

Dodging tourists and keeping an eye out for another wild golf cart, Steven dashed across the street to the shuttle depot. A line of people already snaked through the turnstiles. He managed to bypass a family with a thunderstorm of begging children, colliding with the man in front of him.

"Whoops! Sorry! I seem to be running into all sorts people today."

"No foul done. I can take a few bumps. Howard Line, right?"

"How did you know?"

"It wouldn't seem weird if I said 'clothes make the man,' would it? That's an expensive suit, good tailoring, and those shoes are more at home in the executive boardroom than on a day trip to Catalina. They scream respectability and luxury, and the only cruise line I know that caters exclusively to that is the Howard Line."

"Moonlight as a detective?"

"It's my job to know how much things are worth. I'm in real estate. Name's Josh Cole."

The two shook hands, giving Steven time to appraise the other man's suit. It was less executive, a good cut with cheaper fabric. His shoes were more for comfort than style. His hair gave the illusion that his head was on fire.

"Steven Danforth. And yes, I'm sailing on the Howard Line. I take it you are on the cruise too?"

"Yep. Gift from my sister. She thought my wife and I needed a vacation."

The thunderstorm descended. A thin, adenoidal screech of protest complained about not being able to ride a buffalo. Steven felt a headache prickle at his temples.

"Can't ever escape screaming children, can you? I was hoping to avoid them on this tour."

Josh shrugged and smoothed back his firestorm of hair. "Oh, I don't know. I like kids. I'd like to have some of my own if...if things pan out. Don't mind the noise. If you knew my wife, you'd understand why. Besides, I'm sure that family will sit up front. They're the kind that has to get off first and be close to any guide to ask a million questions. Speaking of which, here's the shuttle."

Josh's prediction came true, as there was nearly an argument with another family about the seating arrangements. The two men decided to seek refuge in the back. In five minutes, the shuttle wormed its way up the mountainside to the Airport-in-the-Sky.

"What business are you in?"

"What was that?"

"Are you enjoying the scenery that much, Steven? I asked 'what business are you in?' I told you I was in real estate."

"Sorry...I had my mind on something else. I work in fashion."

"Hmmm...I pegged you as the lawyering, managing type, not as a designer."

"You're close in your original idea. I'm a business manager for *La Charlegne*. I suppose you've heard of it?"

"Who hasn't? Charlegne Jackson, right?"

"That's the one."

Josh's face pulled itself into a plastic smile. "That...must be interesting."

Steven allowed his eyebrows to reflect his surprise. *Strange...that has to be the phoniest thing I've ever seen. Even phonier than when Charlegne compliments someone.* "It allows me to see something of the world."

"A dot like Catalina Island isn't much of the world."

"I go where I'm wanted."

The adenoidal squeal rose above the road noise in repeated refrains of "I see it! I see it! I see it!"

Josh's lips stretched into a smile. Steven noticed that it looked looser and more relaxed than the other one. "Don't look now, Steven, but I think you've got your chance to escape from family matters."

The shuttle pulled into the parking lot of the Airport-in-the-Sky. The herd of tourists scrambled to the edge of the lot where the landscape fell away into a huge bowl of a valley sprinkled with buffalo. The airport had only one asphalt runway, and the mountainside dropped on either side of it. If a pilot misjudged the landing, his plane would roll right off the cliff.

Steven and Josh skirted the passengers jumbling with their carry-ons and cameras and, chased by the wind chill, hustled into the restaurant, DC-3 Gifts and Grill, in the airport conservatory.

Steven scanned the menu, a frown tugging his lips. "Never been one for buffalo meat. Give me a fatty piece of steak any day. But I guess I'll have the Buffalo Burger everyone is talking about."

"I think I'll have the same, especially since Daphne isn't here to remind me about my cholesterol. Then again, buffalo is supposed to be better for you."

"I hope you don't mind me asking, but why aren't you spending the day with your wife? Why isn't she here?"

Josh's eyes flicked upwards from the menu. There was a second or two of suspicion reflected in them. "I can't see why it's any business of yours."

"I guess it isn't. I was just curious. You speak about her a lot. Newlyweds, I imagine."

"So?"

"So I just wondered why you wouldn't want to spend your day with your wife."

"Oh, Daphne met a woman on the ship and invited her to spend the day together. Sisterhood sort of thing. The lady looked like she needed a break from her steamroller of a husband. Looks on the verge of tears all the time. Daphne knew she needed a friend. Of course, Daphne can make a friend out of anyone. She has that look about her, the friendly, trusting look. I can't describe it that well. Here. I'll show you."

Josh fished his wallet out of his pocket, thumbed through the plastic-sheathed pictures, and drew out the one he wanted. Steven acknowledged it with a faint lift to his eyebrows.

"Oh, I saw her in Avalon. Out in the main street where I had a slight run-in with a golf cart. She came to ask if I was okay. You are certainly a lucky man to have such a pretty wife."

The suspicion returned to Josh's eyes. "What do you mean by that?"

"I believe it was a compliment about your wife."

"Why should you want to compliment my wife?"

"Why are you getting defensive? I just said she was pretty."

"Hey look, pal. I wasn't born under the Stupid Rock. You just asked me why I wasn't with my wife. I'll ask YOU something more interesting. Why were you WITH my wife?"

"I told you I—"

"Don't give me your prearranged bullshit. How could you remember her face after seeing her for just a moment? And what were you doing near her anyway, buddy?"

"I have a good memory for faces. It helps in this business. And I don't need to defend myself."

"The hell you don't! My wife may be a flirt sometimes, but that DOESN'T mean anyone can treat themselves to her! Besides, what the hell would she see in a balding, excessively sweaty piece of driftwood like you?"

Steven's knuckles cracked as he curled his fingers into a fist. "Well thanks for the insults, pal, but I think I'll go choke on my burger in another booth."

Josh shoved the other man back into his seat. "Oh, I'm not done with you yet. I have to lay out some ground rules first."

He's always been a hothead, Steven thought.

"I am not interested in you or your wife. I don't need to stay here and stand trial with a jealous husband."

Josh stopped him with another hard shove. "I'm not jealous! I have no reason to be jealous of a man like you! I'm protecting my wife like a husband should!"

"Hey buddy!" a tourist shouted, his eyes glued to his Instagram page. "Can you keep it down? Some of us are trying to enjoy our lunch!"

Steven scooted out of the booth. "I think you should listen to that man and settle down before you do something stupid."

"So now you think I'm stupid?"

"I hardly know you or your wife!"

"You keep Daphne out of this!"

"You're the one who accused me of doing God-knows-what with her! I wouldn't do a damn thing with someone like your wife!"

Josh lunged at Steven's throat. There was a decidedly feminine screech that threatened to pop eardrums. Steven felt just the flimsiest scratch of fingernails against his neck. He saw an arm cross the angry man's chest and pull him back. Then he recognized the man restraining Josh as Martin Hale, the husband of Charlegne's biggest rival.

"Quit being a moron," Martin advised.

"I'm going to kill him! He can't say that about my wife! I'll kill him!"

"Oh shut up."

"Let me go! I'll—!"

SMACK! The volcano of red curls could only mean one thing—Rosemary. She slapped the furious man hard across the face. It made a sound like a gunshot. The woman who screamed earlier began to yelp like a Chihuahua. Josh shut up and stopped struggling.

Steven thought it best to evacuate.

Across the restaurant, Travis Patrelli stopped tearing through his Buffalo Burger and stared, letting a nugget of half-chewed patty fall from his gaping mouth.

"So, Food Boy, I guess it's just you and me."

Li recoiled. Even his toes curled inside his shoes. Aaron Brent sneered under his fat caterpillar of a mustache. He started to purr.

"I'll be nice to you, kid. I'll have the halibut as is. I won't send it back for anything. I promise." Mr. Brent unzipped a smile that Li hated more than his scowl. "Well, kid? Did you get my order?"

I don't trust you, Mr. Brent.

"Yes, sir. Coming right up."

Li could still see the cold, zipper-like grin frozen on Mr. Brent's face after he turned and walked away.

After delivering the order, Li ran face-first into Paul.

"Oh Christ, Johnson. Can't you watch where you're going, you stupid klutz? At least, you didn't have food in your hands. Charlegne's not here to save her new playmate."

So Travis was right. "Sorry, Paul. I'll try to be more careful."

"You better, or you'll be lucky to be a busboy when I'm through with you, Dropout." Paul chuckled. "Heh, Dropout. I like that. I think that's my new name for you."

You don't want to know what I call you, Paul.

"Halibut's up!"

Li took the steaming dish from the chef and walked out of the kitchen before Paul could levy another insult. Aaron Brent continued to grin that evil, satisfied sneer. Li felt a chill race down the track of his spine.

"Thank you, young man," Aaron purred.

Li stumbled. The fish surfed on a wave of sauce before splattering the champagne suit of the woman at the next table. Her formal arrangement of bronze curls caught the halibut in its net. She rose with a hoarse wail.

Li raced to her side. "I'm so sorry, madam! Please allow me to—!"

She smacked him hard across his face, her fat diamond ring slicing open his cheek. Li began the retreat, staunching the blood with his fingers. The lady then started to shriek at him in a flood of furious French, none of which Li could translate. Paul sprinted to the table, already slipping into his most soothing French platitudes.

Li saw the look on Aaron Brent's face. His beady eyes gleamed like wet onyx. It was pure, gloating satisfaction.

Paul seized the young waiter by his collar and hauled him away, hissing into Li's ear the whole time.

"I have had it with you, Dropout. I hate you. Is that what you want to hear? I hate your guts. You've been one slip-up away from me strangling you this whole trip."

He threw Li into the kitchen and screamed for Chef Will.

Paul held the position of judge and executioner. "The Countess said you purposely threw the food at her, because you have a vendetta against the Swiss."

"That's not true!"

"Don't yell, Dropout!"

"Oh shut up, Paul," Chef Will said. "Instead of lynching Johnson, why don't you ask him what happened?"

"Are you saying that the Countess is lying?"

"Countess Ramseyer has rather fanatical views of the world. She likes to think that everyone has some sort of collective prejudice against the Swiss people, even though she's Swiss by marriage, not birth. I say you give Johnson a chance to tell his side of the story."

"You're willing to let this screw-up defend himself?"

"I believe in fair trial before hanging, Paul."

Paul muttered to himself before turning back to Li. "What happened, Dropout?"

"And for God's sake, Paul, stop calling him Dropout."

"Fine. What happened..." Grinding his teeth together, he squeezed out the name. "...Liam?"

Li didn't respond.

"Out with it, Johnson!"

"He...He tripped me."

"Who did?"

Li hesitated.

"Johnson..."

"A...A customer."

"So you're going to blame someone else—more importantly, a *customer*—for your mistake? I knew you would, you little piece of—"

"Shut up, Paul." Chef Will placed a hand on Li's shoulder. "Now go on and tell us everything."

"I-I'm not really sure of everything. I just remember my ankle hitting something. It...It felt like a foot. Then it all happened so fast. I swear it was an accident! I didn't do it on purpose! Honest!"

He gloated. Mr. Brent gloated at me. He was laughing in his head. This was his plan.

Paul settled a glare on Li that read as "Execution at Dawn." "Countess Ramseyer also insists that you reimburse her for the suit, Johnson. Not dry cleaning. A whole new outfit. I believe it retails for about $2500 American."

Li felt the world spin quickly, and his stomach lurched. "I can't afford that! I can't even afford a new pair of sneakers!"

Paul smirked. "Not my problem. Better whip out your checkbook, Johnson. Or you can start selling yourself on the streets."

"Please, Paul! I'm begging you! I'll be ruined if I have to pay for it!"

"Ruined, eh?"

Chef Will gave the maître d' a hard shove. "Quit being a sadist, Paul. Not even you could afford that suit. The kid's desperate. Why don't you show some damn compassion?"

"The Countess insists that he—"

"Forget the damn Countess. Just have the bartenders at Temptations ply her with those fancy-ass liqueurs she loves so much. She won't even remember the waiter's name after that."

"Nevertheless, this sort of negligence—"

"It was an accident!" Li yelled.

"Accident or not, Johnson, I can't run a dining room if you keep screwing up. Call this your second strike. If you screw up one more time, you're out. For good."

Li appealed to the chef.

"Sorry, Johnson. I run the kitchen. Paul is your boss. If he decides this is the best course of action, well, I'm afraid I can't say much. Just be lucky it's not worse. Now if that's settled, I have a dinner service to organize."

Paul waited until Chef Will's planet of a stomach slipped out of earshot. "I wouldn't feel too safe if I was you, Dropout. You're out of a job. I've already fired you. Once I prove that you slept with Charlegne, you're dead."

Li wasn't listening. His eyes slid out of focus. Something Travis said earlier gave him an idea, an idea to save himself.

A cup of Darjeeling...

CHAPTER 10

Discovery

"Cutting it rather close, aren't we?"

Rosemary accepted the hand of the coxswain as he helped her board the tender. "I guess we are. Our tour ran a little late. Some family with six kids insisted on taking individual shots of all the kids with the bus driver, the buffalo statue, and the waitress who served them. I'm just happy to go back to the ship."

She settled herself in a seat. Martin sat next to her, wrapping his arm around her waist. The tender zoomed toward the ship, kicking up huge feathers of ocean spray.

I lied, Rosemary thought. *I'm dreading going back to the ship. It means going back to her. I can't escape. I tried to...Martin said I was running away. I am trying to run, but I can't get away from her.*

A woman, whose lips seemed incapable of remaining together, began unleashing the thrashing octopus of her hair from its ponytail. "This was a simply wonderful day trip! What a unique island! The Casino had the most colorful and lively murals! Genuine Art Deco, you know!"

These people make me sick. They're just so damn happy.

"And it's a working theater and ballroom! I would love to be there during a big party! With the brass bands and the jazz singers. I could wear that new dress I bought today. Oh, just wait until you see it on me, Josh sweetie. It's the most sumptuous shade of blue, isn't it, Priscilla?"

I hate it! It's impossible to get away! You can see it on all these faces. We can't escape. We will always be drawn back to the ship. Her ship.

"That shade of blue will just make your eyes pop, Daphne. Mr. Cole, you will scarcely recognize your bride when I finish dressing her."

"I look forward to it, Ms. Reilly."

Ugh...why are we are so damn polite? I know these people. They can't stand each other. For instance, over there is Steven Danforth and Priscilla Reilly. They're mortal enemies. And yet, they sit here and play nice to keep up appearances. And it's all for her. They're both slaves to that heartless slut. We're all chained to her in some way.

"Everything all right, Rosie dear?"

"Yes, Marty. Just perfect."

Rosemary glanced at the improbable floating palace inching towards them.

Charlegne's kingdom. It will swallow us alive.

"Oh dear! The spray from the boat got my shopping bags wet! These things wouldn't happen if the boat moved just a teensy bit slower. Wouldn't you say so, girls?"

"Time is everything, Daphne. They can't afford to lag in their schedule."

"Yes," Rosemary said aloud, drawing attention from the passengers around her. "Time is everything. How does that scripture go? 'To everything there is a season, a time for every purpose under the heaven. A time to be born and a time to die...'"

Not even Daphne responded.

"Rosie? Are you sure you're all right?"

"Oh yes, Marty. Everything will be perfect. Much better than before."

The seaborne palace swallowed them at last.

"¡Mi amigo!"

Carlos, one of the stewards, swarmed to Li's side, almost upturning the tea tray Li balanced in his hands. Carlos's thin mustache wriggled as he poured out streams of Spanish that the boy's schoolyard version couldn't possibly grasp.

"¿Es verdad? True, yes? ¿Sabía tu follar Señorita Jackson? Bed? You take to bed? ¿Está todo bien en la cama?"

"NO!"

"Oh? No good?"

"I did not sleep with her!"

"Ohhhhh…¿Es un secreto? Secret, yes? *Mi amigo, tu secreto está a salvo conmigo.* Secret safe here."

Li stressed each syllable. "I…did…not…have…sex…with…her!"

"Ahhhh yes, yes…*Ahora comprendo.* I get you. *Hay muchas mujeres para follar. ¡Muy bien!* Have fun, yes?" Carlos strolled away with laughter exploding out of his throat.

"You should be grateful that you didn't understand what he said, Li." David Kane fell into step beside his bunkmate. "Oh Jesus, Li! What happened to your face? Fist-fight in the dining room?"

"Is it that bad?"

"What the hell happened?"

"I…I had a run-in serving lunch today."

"That's a windfall of information. Out with it, Liam."

"I don't want to talk about it." He stepped up the pace.

David didn't let him escape. "Aw come on…we're bunkmates. I think I have a right to know what happened when the person sharing my quarters has a shiner and a gash on his cheekbone. You're not on the Mob's hit list, are you?"

"I almost wish I was."

"Now stop being morbid and tell me what the hell happened before I dump that tea down your pants."

Li had to stop to tell the story. He didn't think he could pay attention where he was going with his mind otherwise engaged.

"And then after Paul said he had already fired me, I had to go back to the dining room and finish service. Turns out Mr. Brent charmed the Countess into sitting with him and said God-knows-what to her IN PERFECT FRENCH! Last night, he couldn't even pronounce *chateaubriand au poivre!* Now he can suddenly rattle off the most eloquent French I have ever heard! It would make Paul jealous!"

"The guy's a bastard. There's no escaping that."

"Later, I got my shoelace caught in the wheel of the flatware cart and had to sit down to deal with it. The Countess and Mr. Brent used that opportunity to give me two hard kicks in the rear as they were leaving the dining room!"

"I thought you were walking a little funny."

"The worst part was the laughing. At least three tables—and I'm pretty sure Paul—started to chuckle when they did it. Then I had to spend two hours washing all the dishes by myself. I hate this place."

"It's not doing you any favors, that's for sure. Why don't you quit?"

"Why does everyone suggest that I quit? I can't afford to live without this job. And I'm no quitter."

"You're stronger than most, Li. Have to give you that. I really can't believe all the crap Paul and company are giving you about that stupid rumor. Of any guy on this ship, you'd be the last one to bang the Ice Queen. I didn't realize what Jasper meant when he asked what time you returned to our quarters. I made it worse for you, didn't I? If there's anything I can do to make it up to you..."

"Nah. Forget about it. Paul would have jumped on any flimsy excuse to get me fired. I don't blame you."

"Suit yourself. And I thought I was having a bad day."

Li started walking again, the sterling silver teapot clattering on the tray. "What happened to you?"

"Ready for my story, eh? It's not nearly as traumatic as yours, Li. I just haven't been able to stay in one place for very long. I'm a deck attendant that has to moonlight as a steward, a waiter, a tour director, and a personal slave. I'm pretty sure one lady wanted to hire me as her private cabana boy."

"I would have taken the offer."

"Li, at this point, you would agree to be Godzilla's cabana boy. The hard part is directing passengers to people who can actually help them. The usual answer is 'Well, you're here now, so go do what I want!' I have to hunt down a steward to go fetch the crew member the passenger actually needs. I had to entertain this one couple, the Wellingtons, for twenty minutes while Lars chased down the purser. They said it was an emergency. Turns out it was paranoia about the bottled water we provide in all of the cabins. Something about the plastic in the bottle causing cancer. I didn't really listen. Then of course there was the argument I had to break up."

"How come you're the one who gets into fights, but I'm the one with the black eye?"

"Want to trade me places?"

"I'd rather keep both of my eyes, thank you. What happened?"

"Some lady on the Verandah Deck complained about the stewards. Said they liked to play pranks, knocking on her door while she was dressing and then disappearing as soon as she opened it. Something stupid like that. Then she accused them of stealing money from her stateroom. In fact, she held three of them hostage. Bellowed that she wouldn't let 'those slimy bastards' go until she saw the captain."

"Geez. And how did you get involved?"

"I heard her yelling from my post. Her cabin is underneath the ladder. Had to duck a few blows to the head. That woman could bruise a bear just by giving it a pat on the back. She kept us occupied for a good forty minutes while they tried to pry Captain Crayle from the bridge. Eventually, I got her a whiskey and soda, and that seemed to calm her down."

The two men strode through the double doors leading to the Sports Deck, where the sun blistered against their eyes. Li turned toward the Sunbathing Deck. "I'm just ready for this day to be over. I don't think I can take another shock. My system will shut down."

"Then you better take a break after you deliver this tea. Wait...where are you going with this tea?"

"Charlegne ordered it. Lars told me she was up here."

"Aw, you don't have to do that. You've had a rough day, Li. Here, I'll take it for you. Then you can start your break sooner."

"No, it's okay, David. Besides, Charlegne asked for me specifically."

"Far be it from me to stand between Her Majesty and her proclamations."

Li was the first to see her.

Her skin was red. A deep, angry red. She seemed to sizzle in the sunlight. Blisters had bubbled her flesh.

The tray slipped out of Li's hands, making a bright, metallic crash as it hit the deck. He ran to her side and lifted the purple sunhat shading her face.

He met the vacant, dilated gaze of Charlegne Jackson.

"Oh my God..." David's hand clapped over his mouth, muffling his words. His skin flushed the color of algae.

"I...I think she's dead..."

The flashes came then...the hospital...the stink of the antiseptics... the shriveled man with the bloodshot eyes trying not to cry in front of his kids...the old tear stain that exposed him as a liar...the nurses...the doctors...the smell of death...

Li collapsed. David sprinted to the railing and vomited over the edge of the ship.

CHAPTER 11

Death by Sunstroke

I'm back in the hospital. Everything here is so white and clean and perfect. It's like being in heaven...except people suffer here. These antiseptics smell like formaldehyde. They don't save anyone. No one gets cured. They mummify people. And Dad...He's all shriveled and broken...Dad, I'm sorry—I'm sorry I couldn't save you I thought they could make you better and...and...Dad, I miss you so much! I'm so sorry! Please don't hate me! It would kill me if you hated me! Dad, I—!

"Li? Come on, don't scare me like this. Snap out of it."

Li's thoughts seemed to pull away from wet cotton. He blinked and swallowed. The sun roasted his eyeballs.

David seized Li by the shoulders and shook him. "Come on, man. You're starting to freak me out. I don't want to slap you. Li? You still there?"

He blinked again. The white glare started to drain away. "Huh...w-what happened? Where am I?"

"Easy, Li. Take deep breaths. Your name is Liam Johnson. You're on the Sunbathing Deck on the *Excelsior*, a ship on the Howard Line. You work on it as a waiter. Is any of this ringing a bell?"

"David?"

His bunkmate relinquished his breath. "Are you okay? You were really starting to scare me. You just froze. I couldn't get you to respond. You were a zombie. What happened?"

"I...I don't know...I just...blanked. Like I blacked out or something. No, that's wrong. It was a white-out. Everything just went white, like looking into the sun. And...And I was back in the hospital."

"Hospital? What hospital?"

"The...The hospital where my Dad died. He had a really nasty leukemia. Struggled for two years before it finally got him. Today...Well, today is the third anniversary of his death." Li started to shiver.

"He died three years ago today? Oh Jesus, Li. Suffering through that while dealing with all this crap from Paul and the customers. You weren't kidding when you said one more shock would shut down your system."

Li tried to smother the shivers by folding his arms tight against his chest. "I...I d-didn't even realize today was the day he died when I woke up. So many things happened that I didn't have time to stop and think about my dad. It just all piled up. I was living in a haze. Then what happened? It's all fuzzy...I can't...we...we saw her, didn't we?" His eyes ballooned. "Oh God! We saw Charlegne! She was dead! David, she's dead! What are we going to do? Who do we call? Oh God...why is this happening? I can't deal with this! Oh God...I can't...I can't..."

Li crumbled into tears and started to hyperventilate. David barked over his shoulder. "Hey, Doc! I got him to come around, but he's hysterical!"

Li felt cool, professional hands swaddle his hot, tear-soaked cheeks. "Easy does it. Breathe in through your nose and out of your mouth. Deep breaths, nice and slow. Good. Keep it up." Dr. Innsbrook began the routine of checking his pulse. She addressed the two men behind her. "He's in shock."

"Will he be okay?" David asked.

"I think he'll be okay once we get him away from here and he has time to calm down."

"Well, today was the anniversary of his dad's death. Li was always a little depressed and tried to repress his grief. Today was really rough for him. Then...Then we found Charlegne. He just collapsed."

Captain Crayle, bracing himself on the railing and gazing out across the empty sea, allowed himself a slight chuckle. "That's nothing compared to what's going to happen when people find out that she's dead. It seems impossible. I didn't even think you could die that way. It seems impossible."

David addressed the doctor. "How did she die?"

The doctor slipped into her lecturing voice. "Sunstroke."

"Sunstroke?"

The question came from Li. Dr. Innsbrook fussed over her patient. "Just lie still and relax. You don't have to worry."

"I'm okay, Doctor. I think so, at least. What happened to Charlegne?"

"None of your business," the captain snapped. "You are not to breathe a word of this to anyone. Do you all understand me?"

There was a trio of nods.

"Good. I'll return to the bridge. Kane, get two stewards to help you move the...uh...the body into the infirmary. You will make sure it's hidden from passengers, right Doctor?"

"Yes, sir. There's a stretcher behind the large cabinet they can use to move her. We'll put up the curtain around the bed."

"Right. You heard her, Kane. The sooner we clean this up, the better. I'll notify the necessary parties. Remember, not a word of this to anyone. Not one peep, understand?"

The response was affirmative. Captain Crayle plodded down the nearest ladder.

Dr. Innsbrook soon signed off on Li's shock. "Well, you seem to be responding fine. Just take it easy, okay?"

"Yes, Doctor."

"I suggest you rest in your quarters for a bit. Come on, Kane. Let's deal with her."

"Excuse me, Dr. Innsbrook, but...um..."

"Yes?"

"Well...it's just...I mean...can you really die from sunstroke?"

She looked down her nose at Li and opened the lecture. Li could picture her glaring through a pair of pince-nez, shuffling her papers, and haranguing against the evils of skin cancer. "Oh yes. Without much effort. Essentially, it's when you can't get rid of excess heat and your body temperature skyrockets, and you are unable to sweat it off. You pretty much cook your brains."

"How...How long would that take?"

"It depends on many factors. Body type, age, amount of physical activity, weather conditions. Sunstroke can happen anywhere from a half hour to two hours. Which reminds me...how long was she up here, Kane?"

"She came up a few minutes before ten this morning, Doc."

"And you both found her not long after we got underway. So she's been roasting for roughly six and a half hours. Plenty of time."

The algae shade of green flushed David's cheeks again. "Oh God. And I didn't help her. I'm going to be sick. Why didn't I notice something? Why didn't I call for help? Oh my God."

"Don't beat yourself up, David," Li said. "You were constantly distracted by other passengers."

Dr. Innsbrook commanded the lecture again. "It was an awful accident, that's all," Dr. Innsbrook interrupted. "Most people don't know the symptoms of sunstroke. If you don't get immediate medical attention, you could easily die. Saw a case similar to this about five years ago when we went to the Caribbean. A woman decided to catch up on some lost sleep, took a few too many sleeping pills, and passed out on deck. No one noticed anything wrong until she started to burn. We got to her just in time. A very near save. That's why I encourage you to always wear sunscreen, drink lots of water, and wear a hat if you are out in the sun for extended periods."

"Didn't Charlegne do that?"

"No. Her hat lay next to her seat, and there was no sunscreen residue on her body. No bottle near her either. Probably under the misguided notion that she could tan better without it. She paid for it. Come on, Kane. Let's get the stewards. You better get into the shade yourself, Johnson. Don't want you to get sick, too."

The doctor and deck attendant descended the ladder, discussing—of all things—the clear, cloudless sky.

A model that doesn't use sunscreen?

Li wobbled as he heaved himself out of the lounge chair. His legs worked as well as toothpicks. He made slow, stilted steps towards the beautiful, burned figure of Charlegne Jackson.

The red burn contrasted with the golden hair. Li traced her features—her sculpted cheekbones, thin nose, smooth forehead—all of it airbrushed with pink blisters. Her sightless, dilated pupils drilled holes into Li's heart. He remembered the way she looked standing in the dining room doorway last night, skin flushed with fury, her blond hair attacking the air behind her. Now it seemed all that smothered rage, lust, and sorrow boiled on her skin.

No sunscreen anywhere. Dr. Innsbrook was right. But that doesn't make sense.

The only things near her were the fallen sunhat, a beach tote, and a cold cup of coffee on the table to her left. Li's eyes dropped to the shrunken diamond ring on her left hand.

Last night at dinner, her champagne flute sat on her right, and she ate with her fork in her right hand. So why is the coffee on her left? This is getting weirder.

Li sniffed the cold, dark fluid and took an experimental sip. His lips crinkled into a grimace. He started to gag. *Oh yuck! Why do people drink this stuff?* He swished the coffee in his mouth before swallowing it like a child taking his medicine. His stomach revolted. He shivered and wiped his tongue on his sleeve.

Nothing. Just ice-cold, frankly disgusting, black coffee. I'll have to gargle salt water to get the taste out of my mouth. Yecch!

Now feeling genuinely queasy, Li staggered down to the lower decks. He almost tripped and fell when a new thought hit him hard enough to stun his brain.

Dr. Innsbrook said that Charlegne did not wear a hat today, despite its being right next to her chair. That accounts for the burns on her face. But when David and I found her body, her hat shielded her face. I removed it. So who put that hat on her face?

CHAPTER 12

The Necessary Parties

"I can hardly believe what you're telling me, Captain. It just doesn't seem real." Steven Danforth stubbed his half-smoked cigarette in a brass ashtray. His hands trembled. "Charlegne wasn't the type of person who seemed capable of dying. She would live forever in some way. Hell, sometimes even she didn't seem very real. Just some elaborate fantasy." He regretted extinguishing his cigarette. "Are you sure it was Charlegne? I mean, not to speak poorly of your crew, but maybe they had the wrong woman? Mistaken identity?"

"I'm sorry, Steven. I saw her myself. There's no mistake."

"I thought not. You're not the kind of man who makes that kind of mistake." He fumbled in his pockets for the pack he bought in Avalon. "Well...uh...what do you suggest we do, Captain?"

Captain Crayle straightened the centerpiece on the table next to him. "My suggestion is, you wait until we return to Long Beach in two days. You don't want the hassle with the customs people in Mexico trying to get her...her remains back to the States. Patience is the best policy."

"If you think that's best, Captain, then by all means. What sort of... erm...arrangements do we have for her...her body?"

"We've moved her to the infirmary and made sure she is protected from the other passengers. Some of the larger ships have full morgues, but we don't have that luxury."

"That should work out fine. Has anyone told Priscilla Reilly yet?"

"I was going to inform her after I talked to you."

"Good…good…well maybe not so good." Steven drew a fresh cigarette from the box, hesitated, and shoved it back into the pack. "Disgusting habit. You tend to get into some pretty bad ones in this business. Cancer sticks, Priscilla calls them. I've been trying to quit for a while. I guess I won't get that opportunity now that I have to manage—" He loosened his collar with shaking fingers. "This is going to be hell for months."

Damn that woman. Even in death, she makes me miserable. She had to choose the most dramatic exit, too.

The captain, lost in his own troubles, nodded without vigor. "I'm dreading what'll happen when the owners get word of Charlegne's death. They're publicity-shy. Particularly if it's some sort of scandal. God, why couldn't this happen somewhere else?"

"Or to someone else, eh Captain?"

Steven's fumbling fingers dropped his lighter on the floor. The little clunk it made sounded like a bomb in the near-empty smoker's lounge.

The captain sighed. "She was a beautiful woman."

"I suppose she was."

"God doesn't make many Charlegne Jacksons."

"I guess not."

She was too beautiful to die. Like Crayle said, God's hands crafted that. And no one less than the Almighty Himself could have destroyed the beauty He created. He used the only thing that shined brighter than she did. The sun. He destroyed my Lena with the single brightest star in our sky.

"We're in for one hell of a storm, Steven. Hope you have a good set of sea legs for this one. It's going to get ugly."

Ugly…everything that Lena wasn't. How ironic.

"I'll be ready when it comes, Captain."

Captain Crayle stood and continued to fuss with the placement of the ashtrays and centerpieces. Steven suppressed a smile at this open display of the captain's domestic worries. "When we reach port, naturally there'll be complications. The police will want statements, just as a formality. You and Ms. Reilly will have to remain on the ship for a while after we dock."

"I understand."

"That's settled then."

Settled. That's how we like our problems. Everything has to be neat and precise, swept under rugs. God forbid anything should be left as a loose end.

We're not like Lena. She could keep a wound open for life. And she did. It was her favorite pastime.

"I better go inform Ms. Reilly and return to the bridge."

"Allow me, Captain. You have a ship to run. I'll break the news to Priscilla."

"Thanks, Steven. And don't worry. We'll put a lid on the chatter. Not a soul knows about Charlegne's death except for the ship medic, you, soon-to-be Ms. Reilly, a couple of the ship's staff, and me. We won't let it get around. We don't need the extra headache."

It'll be a headache anyway, Captain. Just hide and watch.

"We can only do our best."

The captain strode out of the smoker's lounge. Steven bent down and picked up his fallen lighter. Then he removed a fresh cigarette from the pack, pinched it between his lips, and lit it. He burned through the whole thing on one drag and tried to exhale his memories.

"And then Rosemary Hale just WAILS one right across the guy's face! His whole left cheek glowed red. Like a really bright sunburn. If she hit him as hard as the Countess hit you, Li, you're both going to have matching shiners this time tomorrow."

Travis laughed so hard that he knocked one of the polished martini glasses off the bar.

"Mrs. Hale did that?" Li asked.

"Hell yes! We always knew she had a fire brewing inside her. Lord, you should have seen the look on this guy's face, Li. I think he crapped his pants a little. One good bitch slap and he stopped. He certainly didn't shout murder after that."

"Wow. Everyone's going crazy on this trip."

"We can call it the Catfight Cruise. Charge people for tickets to see the rich beat the tar out of each other. Now that's a million-dollar return on investment. All we'd really need to do is throw Charlegne and Rosemary in a room and lock the door."

Li choked a little on his water.

"So...um...what happened to the other guy?"

"Who?"

"The man who was accused of...well...I don't really know what...with the guy's wife?"

"Oh, him. He scuttled out of the restaurant as quickly as he could. I saw him chain-smoking out by the buses a few minutes later. I guess everything proved to be too much for his reserved, professional exterior." Travis started to whistle. "So when will Paulie let you back in the dining room?"

Li drained the rest of his water in one gulp. "What makes you think Paul even wants me in the dining room?"

"Is that a 'never again'?"

"Something like that. He told me not to show up until an hour before service. I have another thirty minutes to waste."

"I guess he's trying to Li-proof the dining room as much as he can." When he saw his friend's scowl, Travis rolled up his polishing rag and whacked Li on the arm with it. "Oh, don't be so sour, Li. It's just a joke."

"Paul will be the only one laughing if dinner doesn't go perfectly for me. I can't let him or Mr. Brent or anyone run me over for their personal enjoyment."

"Better work on your reflexes and daring acrobatics, my friend."

Li grumbled under his breath.

"Someone is crankier than usual. Does this have anything to do with your dad?"

"Partly."

"Well, come on, man. Spill."

"Why do you think there's anything else that's wrong? I had a bad day."

"You've been downing water as if hoping you can get drunk on it. Sorry Li...I didn't spike your glass with anything harder. So tell me what's on your mind."

"I can't."

"Why not?"

"I just can't, Travis."

"That's not one of your more creative excuses."

"Look, I can't tell you because the captain forbade me to tell anyone."

Travis stopped polishing, pocketed the rag, and plunked a bottle of vodka in front of his friend. "I will get you so drunk, and you will spill every last secret in your head. Unless of course, you want to save me the trouble and my job. I think I know which one you prefer, Li. Spill it."

Li shoved the bottle aside. "Why do you want to know so badly?"

"You mentioned the Captain. That means something big. Really big. Now, I remember you suddenly choking when I mentioned Charlegne and Rosemary. It's one of them, isn't it? I really can't see it being Rosemary. I saw her on the island. So I'm guessing it was the self-proclaimed empress." His eyes bore into Li's face. "Well? Was it Charlegne?"

"I told you. I can't talk about it."

"I knew it. It was Charlegne."

"I didn't say anything!"

"You didn't say 'no' either."

"I'm getting out of here. Maybe I can beg Paul to let me in early."

Travis pulled Li back into his seat. "What happened? Did you catch the captain having sex with her? Did he order you to keep the whole thing under wraps or you'd lose your job? There was always that rumor..."

"Let me go, Travis!"

"Or maybe that rumor Jasper spread was true, and you were lying to save yourself. Is that what happened, Li? Did Captain Crayle catch you and Charlegne having a little too much summertime fun?"

"NO!"

"Did he threaten to get rid of you? Did Charlegne beg and plead to save the little what's-his-face she likes to fool around with?"

"Nothing happened between us!"

"I wondered, you know. You deserved a break from the ship, and yet, you chose to stay behind. Charlegne wanted you there, didn't she? DIDN'T SHE?"

Li shoved Travis away from him. The bartender backed into the glass shelves behind the bar. The bottles clattered and trembled, and one wine glass fell to join its cousin on the floor.

"When will you get it through your thick head that I have done nothing wrong? I'm being victimized here! Paul is one thing, but I thought YOU were my friend, Travis! How could you accuse me of doing anything to Charlegne? I didn't know her! I know nothing about her! How could you treat me like I'm some disgusting man-slut who goes behind people's backs and has sex with their secret fantasy girls? Don't you know anything about me?"

Something like latent electricity hummed in the air. Both men panted heavily.

"Get out, Li. Get out of my bar. If you can't trust me enough to tell me what's going on...."

"I told you a dozen times! I CAN'T TELL ANYONE!"

"Shut up, Li. As I was saying, if you don't trust me, then I don't want to deal with you or your problems or your stupid father."

Li snapped. "DON'T YOU DARE CALL MY FATHER STUPID!"

"Boy, what got into you, Johnson?"

Li stopped polishing and throwing silverware into the black plastic tub at his side. It looked like he had been shocked awake from a dream.

"Oh...uh...what do you mean?"

Marisol scratched at some stain on a knife with a long acrylic nail. "You look like you're stocking up on weapons for a war. You just grab a fork or whatever, polish it, and fling it in the bucket. Scowling the whole time, too."

"I...I had a bad day."

"Try not to take it out on the silverware. Flying knives should stay in the circus." The room service line screamed into life. Marisol picked up the receiver. "I'm sorry, but the kitchen is closed until service begins at seven. What? Oh, okay. Johnson, it's for you."

"Are you the one who delivered Miss Jackson's breakfast this morning?" barked the woman at the other end.

"Yes, madam."

"Come pick up this filthy breakfast tray! Next time, don't be lazy and leave it behind!"

"Very well, madam."

He handed back the receiver without confirming which stateroom.

"If Paul cares enough to ask, tell him I went to pick up a tray from a passenger's cabin."

"Oh, so I have to take orders from you now?"

Li ground his teeth together. "Please, Marisol. I'm in a lousy mood, and I really don't want to start yelling at people."

"Oh, shut up and get out of here. I'll cover your ass, if I have to."

Li stormed to the service elevator, grumbling under his breath.

He hesitated when he saw the "Do Not Disturb" sign on the door of Charlegne's cabin. He listened. There was no sound from the cabin. Li knocked, and the sounds of sobbing began. It was like someone inside the room waited for an audience. He shook the thought out of his head.

The door opened enough to reveal a bloodshot eye rimmed with tears.

"I'm here to pick up the tray."

The eye withdrew, and the crack widened. Li crept into the cabin. Huddled in some odd, black, hooded caftan on the bed was Priscilla Reilly, dabbing away tears with a soiled handkerchief.

"I'm sorry," she muttered. "I didn't want to be seen like this. It's just... the news about Charlegne."

Li hesitated, but then placed his hand on her shoulder. "I understand. I...I found her."

"You? Oh my God...but you're so young. And to find her...oh, you poor boy..."

"I'm okay. It...It wasn't the first death I've seen."

"I just can't imagine what we'll do without her." She floated toward the dressing table, the flowing folds of fabric eclipsing her feet. The whole outfit gave her an almost religious air. *Like a nun*, Li thought.

"I suppose I should grab the tray and get out of your way." His eyes fell on an open suitcase tightly packed with designer clothes. "You...uh... seem to be busy."

"Just making sure her...her belongings are packed." She fell into her private worries and mumbled aloud. "I can't think where that bottle could be. She never sunbathed without it."

"Ma'am?"

"What? Oh...I'm sorry...I was...distracted. The t-tray is on this dressing table. I can't think why it was left behind."

Li refrained from mentioning the "Do Not Disturb" sign dangling from the doorknob.

"I'll take care of it."

"This is a terrible tragedy! I don't know if I can even stomach the idea of dinner. There's just so much to take care of and...Oh, Charlegne!" Priscilla threw herself on the bed and began another spurt of crying. Vibration from the impact toppled a small bottle of sleeping pills on the nightstand, throwing the tiny white tablets onto the floor like rice at a wedding.

"Will you be okay?"

"I-I just need to b-be alone." She lifted her head, and the image of a nun weeping at an altar intensified in Li's mind. "Y-You can go now. Thank you for c-coming so promptly. I...I don't think I'll be at dinner tonight. Don't wait for me."

"Shall we send up some food for you later?"

"No...No...I'd get sick at the sight of food, right now. Please go."

Li stumbled over a loose, rubber doorstop and nearly pulled a groin muscle trying to keep the carefully balanced coffee cup from sliding off the tray. He kicked the doorstop out of his way, and it scuttled under the bed. With a final farewell, he left the cabin and collided into a wall of a woman.

"Oops! I'm sorry! I—"

"I caught you at last, sonny! Thought you could get away with it this time, didn't you? I'll have your superiors on your ass for this!"

"I-I didn't do anything!"

The giant woman lifted Li by the collar of his white button-up shirt. His toes dangled at least three inches off the ground. "Oh yeah? Do you think it's decent to interrupt a woman while she's dressing for dinner? Do you all think it's funny to knock on a lady's door and run off? I have news for you, sonny! It's rude and perverted!"

"I-I-I'm sorry, Miss—"

"It's Mrs. Anderson to you!"

"I'm sorry, Mrs. Anderson. I-I didn't mean to bother you. But I didn't knock on your door and—"

Mrs. Anderson dropped him. Li crashed to the ground, the falling tray bellowing like a dinner gong. The empty coffee cup he tried to salvage earlier shattered into porcelain confetti.

"Don't give me your excuses! I know what I heard! Two beats. Sharp. Short. A steward's knock. Just like I heard this morning."

"I-I-I'm sorry. It won't happen again, Mrs. Anderson."

"If it does, I'm holding YOU accountable, sonny! Now get out of here!"

Mrs. Anderson thundered back to her stateroom.

Before he could get up, the cabin door next to Charlegne's opened and slammed into Li's shin. He bit down on his lip to stifle a swear word. He looked up in time to see Sally Brent peek around the door and dart back inside her stateroom in half of a heartbeat.

Li couldn't forget the terror scratched into Sally's face.

CHAPTER 13

The Missing Sunscreen

"Look at that, Sally. These young snots are always getting into fights at work. The kid's got a black eye, a cut on his cheek, and a limp. Probably thinks he's some big tough stud. Watch me tear him down a couple of notches. Hey Food Boy! Get your ass over here!"

Li limped to the table, wishing he could just drop dead from the strain.

"Someone had a productive day, eh Food Boy?" Aaron Brent let a laugh tear open his mouth. It made Li think of boulders gnashing and crashing against each other.

"Are you ready to order, sir?"

"Are you trying to hurry me along, kid? Worried about what mean, nasty trick I'll play on you tonight?"

Yes, Mr. Brent. I'm worried. It might be safe to say I'm scared of you.

"I can give you a few more minutes if that's what you need."

Aaron snatched Li's wrist. "Oh, I'm not done with you, kid. We're going to have some fun, okay? How does that sound?"

Sounds like murder, Mr. Brent.

"I...I can give you a few minutes to decide while I—"

"Are you scared, kid? You're looking a little pale."

"I-I can recommend the lobster with—"

"You know, I heard some gossip among your coworkers that you are on thin ice with your boss. One more mistake and you lose everything."

"Aaron, honey—"

"Be quiet, Sally. I'm going to handle this. So, kid, if I were to accuse you of poor service, how long would it take to get you to cry and grovel at my feet? How badly do you need this gig? If I caused a scene right now, how long before you are homeless on the streets and chewing on cardboard for food?"

"I...I...I..."

"You what, kid? You hate me? You're sick of me? Go ahead. Say whatever you want."

His eyes gleamed like black marbles. He purred again.

Li felt the bottom of his stomach plunge.

"A-Are you ready to order, sir?"

Aaron's face settled back into a scowl. He released his hold on Li's wrist. "Lamb. Cook it through. Extra sauce. And send that stupid Wine Guy over here. I'm going to need some strong red to swallow this swill. Sally. Order."

Sally Brent stopped shredding a dinner roll with her fingernails. "The...The quail, please."

"Well, Food Boy? Are you happy now?"

"Coming right up, sir."

"Good. Now get out of my sight."

Li fled. He didn't stop until he disappeared into the kitchen.

Chef Will turned around and nearly knocked Li over with his belly. "You look like you've seen a ghost, Johnson. Or did you piss off Paul?"

"What? Oh...uh...I...I'm fine." He delivered the Brents' order.

"We'll deal with that. Right now, you need to get your butt to the Captain's Table. It seems Her Royal Highness and her two servants decided against having dinner in MY dining room. Good riddance. Now I can finally start serving dinner when I want to. Get going, Johnson!"

"I thought Paul said I was banned from the Captain's Table if Charlegne wasn't there?"

"Do you really need to ask for reasons? It seems you're able to charm fashion designers. Word is Rosemary Hale insisted you continue to serve at her table. Anyway, who cares why they did it? Your butt is supposed to be out there right now. Here's the amuse-bouche. Get moving!"

Li sped to the Captain's Table, thankful to see Paul attending to customers across the dining room. He presented the menu himself.

"Is everything all right this evening?" Rosemary asked, nibbling at the surgically stacked bite of food on a golden spoon.

Li topped off her wine glass. "Yes, Mrs. Hale. Is there anything I can help you with?"

"I...I just noticed that Charlegne isn't here. She usually loves to make an entrance. Is she okay?"

Li noted that Martin watched his wife with his eyebrows pinched tightly together.

"We received word that she was not attending dinner in the dining room. Can I get you anything else, Mrs. Hale?"

"Oh...um...no...No, I think I'm fine. Thanks."

"Oh Fooooooooooooooood Booooooyyyyyyyyy!!! I'm staaaaaaaaaaarving!"

When Li served the entrées, Aaron stabbed his wife's quail with a steak knife.

"This looks underdone. Wouldn't you say so, dear?"

Sally looked like she was asked to drown a child.

"Oh...oh no...No, it looks—"

"Underdone, Sally. Isn't it?"

"Oh...I...I-I don't..."

Aaron's scowl sank into his wide, red face. "Are you going to let this punk serve you poisoned slop, dear?"

"Aaron, I—"

"Send it back."

"If you'll allow me to take your plate, madam—"

"Shut up, Food Boy. Sally. Do it."

Sally pushed away her plate with her fingernail. Her face seemed to shrink behind the dingy veil of her hair. Li took the plate and turned, catching only a scrap of their conversation.

"You didn't play along, Sally."

"Aaron, I—"

"Shut up, Sally."

"You know I hate seeing you return with untouched food, Johnson." Chef Will let the quail slide into the trash can. "What was it this time?"

"They said it was undercooked."

"We're going to run out of food before we reach Mexico at this rate. Take the first course to the Captain's Table."

Before Li could even move his hand to touch the food cart, Paul barreled into the kitchen. "Don't touch that, Dropout. You'll just make a mess. I'll take it. You go get some more napkins from the storeroom. Now!"

Li jerked his lips into a toothy smile. "Right away, sir!"

"No one likes a kiss-ass, Dropout."

The napkins were easy to find. Li turned to leave when he heard his name on the other side of the storeroom door.

"Do you think the rumor about Johnson and Charlegne Jackson is true?"

"Damned if I know. Johnson denies it, but that's what I would do in that situation, wouldn't you? And then there was this whole 'It wasn't her cabin' thing. How would he know something like that? He's always acted a bit funny."

Li held his breath and listened closer.

"What do you mean, Jer?"

"He's always moping about, looking miserable. Keeps to himself a lot. Quiet. I know we're not exactly friends or anything, but I don't really care for the overly quiet people. They're creepy, Ross."

"I know what you mean, Jer. Johnson can be a weirdo sometimes. Like when he does his homework."

"Homework? I thought he dropped out of college?"

"He did. That's what's so weird about it. He left school, but still studies?"

Li ground his teeth together. *I dropped out because the school kept cutting classes I needed, and my family's income and savings totally dried up. I still study because I don't want to fall behind.*

"But that's nothing compared to what I just heard, Ross!"

"What is it?"

"Johnson found Charlegne's dead body."

"Aw, come on! Don't pull my leg!"

"I'm serious! I heard it from a steward! The Ice Bitch is dead!"

"How?"

"Dunno. Nobody really knows. But it's true. The story is floating around the whole ship. Apparently, they're going to plan some stupid memorial for her."

"Geez. I didn't think she could ever die."

"Yep. And I'll tell you something else: I think Johnson killed her."

Li could feel his heartbeat in his teeth.

"What the hell are you talking about, Jer?"

"Do I have to spell it out? First, Charlegne demands that Johnson serves her table. Then there's this whole rumor about Johnson having sex with Charlegne. Then he conveniently finds her dead body!"

"But still—"

"I bet the rumor was true. I bet you a week's pay that Charlegne 'invited' Johnson to her cabin after dinner. He goes at the appointed time, and they do the nasty. But it doesn't stay a secret like he hoped it would. Word has it that he can't afford to lose his job. What if she says something that could ruin everything for him? So he kills her. She may have even left him a substantial wad of greenback in her will. They may have known each other beforehand for all we know. That's why she demanded he serve her table."

"Wow...Crazy..."

"I'll find out of course. No one will pay much attention to a waiter snooping. I'll have to find out how he killed her. Maybe he slipped something in that tea he said he delivered to her. We'll have to be careful, Ross. He might be a psychopath."

Li felt his jaw tense like a stretched rubber band. *I hate these people*, he thought.

"Boy, Jer, you could be another Sherlock Holmes."

"Hey, if the cruise ship business doesn't work out, I could start my own P.I. agency!"

Maybe if you get your head out of your butt first.

"We better get back to the dining room before Paulie throws us off the ship with Johnson."

"Paulie wants to chuck Johnson?"

"Aren't you the amateur detective, Jer? Paulie can't wait to dump him. He hates Johnson. Super jealous of all the attention he gets. He's just waiting to prove that Johnson slept with Charlegne, so he can fire him."

"Maybe I can help Paulie out. I certainly don't want to work with a murderer. And keep up your poker face, Ross. Johnson's out there. Don't let him on to the fact that you know his secret."

Footsteps stretched into silence. Li stumbled out of the storeroom. His blood pounded in his head.

They all want to get rid of me. Everyone wants me to lose my job, to lose everything I have! What am I going to do?

"Christ, what took so damn long?" Paul ripped the cloth napkins out of Li's grip. "Remember, Dropout, one teeny tiny mistake and you're out of here for good. You'll be drinking water out of the gutters when I'm done with you. Get your ass to Table 12! I'll handle the Captain's Table this evening."

"Yes, sir."

He shuffled back into the dining room. At Table 12, Li found Countess Ramseyer. He felt like hanging himself with a tablecloth.

"I'll have ze cod," she muttered.

He returned with the steaming entrée. The countess acknowledged it with an elegant grunt. Once he turned around, he felt something searing hot and wet splatter all over his back. His ear burned. He looked down to see a white lump of fish bleeding sauce into the carpet.

That's it! I'm done! I hate this ship! I hate these people! I hate everything here!

Li popped on a plastic smile and turned to the Countess.

"Shall I get you another cod, madam?"

Sally Brent was in her garden again. Over the cold, dry years, her mind wove the wrought-iron into the curls of a garden gate, stitched grass into the earth, and draped the brick walls with a wild rainbow of impossible flowers. Sally crept around the Forbidden Ones, the eroding stone statues of people from her past, people she had been ordered to no longer see in real life. She stroked their tear-worn features with her thumb, trying to dredge up the face that matched. Her memories were as fragile as interrupted dreams.

Back in reality, Sally stumbled around the ship's Atrium, comatose to the chaos of the passengers and crew.

There was a new statue in the secret garden. One whose features time hadn't yet buffed away. Sally recognized the freshly whittled face of Charlegne Jackson. She didn't need to dredge deep for these memories. It was the woman who saved her, the woman who made her life all the more agonizing.

How could she do this to me?

Outside the garden, Sally twisted her split ends into a thick rope of hair and teetered into the glass elevator.

Already Charlegne's stone effigy started to blur with tears. Sally couldn't feel that the tears were her own, but she could see a dim reflection of her pain in the classic elegance of Charlegne's features.

The elevator's bright ping signaling the end of her journey shocked her out of the fantasy. She couldn't recall ever pushing the elevator button. Her life was pure muscle memory. With a wooden gait, Sally shuffled down the passageway of the Verandah Deck. She tried to fall back into her secret garden. She could see the dream flowers scale the walls around her. They grew black and oily before melting into a bad taste in her mouth.

She neared the source of the poison. The swirls in the pattern of the carpet twisted and stretched toward a distant door—her cabin door. Her tears evaporated. She couldn't risk Aaron seeing her cry without cause. Especially, if he didn't cause it.

The lock slurped up the keycard. Her fingertips stuck to the doorknob. It turned smoothly.

Sally knew this was a fatal mistake.

"Where were you, dear?"

Aaron sat in the wingback chair across from the door. Hate darkened his face.

"Where were you, Sally?"

"I...I went for a short walk."

"Where?"

"Around the Atrium."

"Were you with anyone?"

"N-No."

"Don't lie to me, dear."

He only used "dear" when he wanted her to do something. Or when he wanted to suck the air out of her lungs.

"I met no one, Aaron."

Aaron's whole body scowled at her. "You abandoned me today, Sally."

"Aaron, I—"

"Shut up. You left me. Several times. That primped prostitute last night. That stupid woman who couldn't stop yammering this morning. They took you away from me, Sally. You know how I feel about that."

"Aaron, honey—"

"You begged to come on this cruise. It was your idea. And you're using it as an opportunity to get away from me. After all I've done for you."

"Please, Aaron, I—"

"I said 'Shut. Up.'"

Sally did.

"I've had my own fun, dear. I tried not to take it out on you. You should be grateful."

Sally said nothing.

"But it wasn't enough. Sure I had fun, but that wasn't the point. I may have dealt with some of the annoyances, but I didn't get to the heart of the problem."

Sally tried to shrink into the carpet.

"You."

Aaron Brent unbuckled his belt and yanked it through the belt loops in one hard tug. It hissed at Sally. Her husband held up the belt for her to examine: the tense leather, the sharp fangs of the buckle.

"Shut the door, dear."

She hesitated. There was a small chance. She could turn...run...scream. Surely a passenger or a member of the crew would hear her. They would know. They would take her away from Aaron. She would be free.

"Shut. The. Door."

There was psychic pull in those black cobra eyes.

Her hands fumbled like clumsy spiders over the doorknob.

Her throat closed in tandem with the door.

"Look at me, Sally."

Her eyes flicked upwards.

"You don't play along, dear. And we know what happens to people who don't play along. Get on the bed."

"Oh please, Aaron! I'm sorry! I'll never do it again! I'll never leave your side! Please don't! You always make it hurt! I'm—"

The belt cracked across her face, sounding loud enough to start a revolution. Fireworks of pain exploded along her jaw. He only hit her with the leather. That was good.

"Get. On. The. Bed."

Sally's feet felt weighed down with sand, but she heaved forward. Her eyes started to get wet, but she sucked back on the tears to keep them from falling. To her, it looked like the bed floated on a floor of tears.

"Face down. You know I hate to see you cry."

She prostrated herself on the white bed linen.

"You have to learn, Sally dear. I'm sorry."

She hated when he apologized.

Sally buried her face into the pillow, praying that this time she would just die.

"Homework again?" David asked.

Li's stormy blue eyes peeked over the tattered cover of his math workbook. "Is there a reason I can't do homework?"

"Don't you get cramps if you do it immediately after a horrible dinner service?"

"This one wasn't that bad."

"Then how do you explain that burn on your left ear?"

Li brushed his ear with the tips of his fingers and winced. "Would you believe me if I said I got into a hideous accident with a Baked Alaska?"

"At this point, yes, I would." David bookmarked his thriller novel and tossed it on top of Li's copious notes, which earned him a sour look from his bunkmate. He stretched out his legs and scanned the crew lounge. "Why are you studying anyway, Li? I thought you had to leave school?"

Li disappeared behind his workbook again. "I wanted a distraction."

"About your dad?"

Li grumbled.

"Or about Charlegne?"

"What makes you think I have any memories of her?"

"Well, I hate to bring it up, but we did find her body."

Li shushed him. "You heard the Captain, David! We're not supposed to—"

"Oh relax." David gestured to the crew members reaching second base on the sofa. "Even if Carlos came up for air, he barely understands English."

"I don't want anything to risk my job. I'm already dealing with a psychotic boss and his hair-trigger temper. I'm just going to keep my head down and serve people whatever they want. Perfect little waiter." Li plunged under the safe umbrella of the quadratic formula.

David pushed the spine of the workbook down so he could look Li in the eye. "Then I suggest you come clean about a certain tea delivery you made."

Li fought the urge to throw the workbook across the lounge. His voice struggled to stay smooth. "I did not—repeat DID NOT—have sex with—"

"Not that delivery, doofus. The later one. The one you were making when we found Charlegne's body."

The apples of Li's cheeks went pink. "I...um...I..."

"The truth would be nice, Li. I don't think you have time to come up with a lame excuse."

"You can't prove that there was something fishy about me delivering tea to Charlegne this afternoon!"

"Are you sure about that, buddy? Last night, Charlegne ordered Oolong tea. When I saw you in the passageway this afternoon, you said you were delivering tea to Charlegne. The tea was Darjeeling. I know Charlegne's habits. She doesn't change her tea preferences at the drop of a hat. And even if she did, she would have asked me, the deck attendant waiting on her, to serve her, no matter how much she liked you. So you were clearly lying."

"I-I don't have to defend myself!"

David sent a few sentences of perfect Spanish over his shoulder towards the couple on the couch. Li's classroom version barely caught the word *escuchar*, meaning "listen." He tugged on David's shirt sleeve.

"Okay! Just don't get other people involved, please?"

"I thought that would get your attention."

"Not funny."

"I'm not laughing, Li. Now spill before I grow old and die in this seat."

Li glanced at the overheated couple before starting to talk. "I didn't do anything with Charlegne if that's what you're thinking. But when Paul said he would stop at nothing until he proved that I slept with her, I panicked. I know he couldn't prove it definitively, seeing as nothing happened, but I was terrified he might be able to twist something innocent and convince certain people in charge that I did sleep with her. I freaked out. I needed a character witness, someone who could clear my name. And the only person I could think of with that kind of power was Charlegne herself. My friend, Travis, joked that I needed her to fake cry and drink Darjeeling while defending my character. It got into my head.

I got the tea and said Charlegne ordered it. I didn't even remember the actual kind she liked. The image of a cup of Darjeeling just stuck. I needed an innocent excuse to see her and beg her to help me. I was desperate." Li's shoulders drooped. "Then...Then we found her."

"Yeah. Bummer."

"You believe me, don't you?"

"Yeah, I do. Now that you've actually told me the truth." David leaned back and balanced his chair on two legs. "Guess you're kind of screwed now that Charlegne is out of the picture. What'll you do?"

"I can try to find out who did sleep with her and see if he would be willing to help me."

"That's asking a lot of a man willing to sleep with the Queen of the Cold Shoulder."

"Maybe. It's either that or get hanged as Charlegne's boy toy."

"There are worse titles."

Li's pencil trembled as he scrawled a few shaky numbers on his scratch paper. "Things would be so much easier if Charlegne hadn't...hadn't died. It seems impossible. If I didn't see it for myself." His eyes swelled, pushing his eyebrows higher up his forehead. He raked his hand through his black hair in quick swipes. "Someone must have seen her."

David let his chair fall back onto four legs and checked his bunkmate's forehead for a fever. "What the hell possessed you this time, Li? If you slip into shock again, I'll take a risk and slap you."

"Someone had to have seen her besides you, David. Maybe this morning before the tenders left for Catalina Island."

"I don't doubt that."

"Did you see anyone near the Sunbathing Deck around the time Charlegne got there?"

David fiddled with his collar. "I'm not sure I should mention any names. That could cost me my job."

"Well, they might have seen what Charlegne did this morning and whether she did anything different from her normal routine."

"What makes you think she did anything different?"

Li thought of the missing sunscreen. "Oh...no special reason..."

"You're lying again."

"You have to admit that someone like Charlegne Jackson didn't seem like a person who would die suddenly."

"Just because it seemed like that doesn't mean it's impossible."

"Well yes, but—"

"But what, Li? What are you hinting at this time?"

Li began folding and unfolding a corner of his workbook. He kept his eyes glued to the equations stamped onto the paper. "A model would use sunscreen."

"So?"

"So she would take the necessary precautions. I don't think she would forget, and it's even less likely that she would refuse to use it on purpose."

"I can't see how that's important."

"I guess it isn't, but it might be good to find out what she did." He added quickly: "For the people who joined her on this cruise. Maybe it will make them feel better to know that it wasn't something else."

David arched an eyebrow. "You're not going to do something stupid, are you?"

"Depends on your definition of stupid."

"There goes the other eye. Try not to get yourself killed, okay?"

"I think I'm smarter than that."

"That remains to be seen." David pinched his eyelids together and rubbed his forehead. "I can see you getting into trouble already. Don't mention my name, okay?"

"I wouldn't do that."

"Well...I did see some passengers in the vicinity. Three total. They were...um...You're sure that you won't—?"

"I promise, David. I won't drag you into this."

"Okay, I guess. Martin Hale sat near the pool, looking toward the Sunbathing Deck. He's the husband of Rosemary Hale, the fashion designer. They both sail frequently with the Howard Line. Rosemary was at the opposite end, standing at the Prow Deck."

He paused.

"But who was the third person?"

"I don't know. I mean I don't know her name. She's not a regular. She sat next to Mr. Hale and never stopped talking. She burned through more words than I have ever heard in my life. I thought Mr. Hale would fall into a coma from listening to that."

"Did this woman have a lot of unruly black hair?"

"It was black all right, and I guess you could call it unruly." David's eyes narrowed. "Why did you ask?"

"I just had a thought. Are you sure you didn't recognize her?"

"I never saw her sail on the Howard Line before this trip. She's not one of the passengers whose names I'm supposed to remember."

"Like Charlegne Jackson?"

"Exactly."

"And you would know about the people associated with Charlegne?"

"I'm really nervous about what you're getting at, Li. Can you just quit this amateur investigation and go back to your life as an unassuming waiter?"

Li hedged the question, busily rubbing away a few errant pencil marks with his eraser.

David snatched the workbook from Li. "You're avoiding the question, which means you're hiding something."

"You wouldn't want to hear it anyway."

"If you're about to stick your neck into a noose on my information, I have a right to know who the hangman is."

"Well, a woman ordered me to remove a forgotten tray in Charlegne's cabin. I just wondered who she was. I gathered she worked for Charlegne."

"Did she dress in weird clothes? Like big, ugly tents?"

"I don't know about the ugly part, but yeah."

"It had to be Priscilla Reilly, Charlegne's lead assistant. Also known as a yapping, snob-pleasing, unstylish doormat. Why? What's so important about her?"

"I get a weird vibe from her."

"Everyone does. It's because she practically licks the floor clean before Charlegne's delicate feet can even dare touch it."

"It's partly that." Li tapped his pencil on the tabletop in an effort to drown out the sounds of suction coming from the lounge sofa. "But there's something odd about Ms. Reilly." He explained in further detail what happened in Charlegne's stateroom.

His bunkmate grimaced. "I think you're getting a little fanciful, Li. I can't see anything weird in that."

"It was just the way everything made me feel. The loud sobbing that didn't start until after I knocked...throwing herself on the bed and bawling...the way she dressed..."

"What was special about her clothes?"

"It made her look...kind of like a nun." *Almost like she was forcing the impression that she was a woman deeply and spiritually hurt by her employer's death,* he added inwardly.

"I grant you that Priscilla Reilly has as much fashion sense as a fence post, but I don't understand your point. And that worries me because I have this weird, shaky feeling that you're going to do a lot of stupid and dangerous things before this trip is over."

Li didn't respond immediately. The sucking noise from the couch magnified in volume. It was an ugly, invasive sound.

"Like I said, it depends on your definition of stupid."

David grabbed Li by the shoulder, digging his thumb under his bunkmate's collarbone. "You're not going to CONFRONT these people I mentioned, are you? That's like suicide on this ship! Are you crazy?"

Li started to pack up his school supplies. "I'd like to stay and discuss my pending insanity with you, but I have to see someone."

"Oh for God's sake, Li! Don't be an idiot! You just said that you can't afford to lose this job! Well, what you're doing right now is equivalent to using Paul's shoes as a surrogate toilet!"

"I'm not going to confront any of them, David. I'd like to think I still have part of a brain in my skull."

"I'm getting less confident in that the more you talk, Li."

"Thanks, bunkmate. That lifts my spirits enormously." Li rolled his eyes and turned to leave, but David caught him by his sleeve.

"Just one second, Mr. Nut Job. Who exactly are you going to see anyway?"

"I have to see a doctor about a sunburn."

"Are you sure you only work in the dining room, Johnson? These injuries are more at home with a bare-knuckled pugilist than a waiter."

Li worried that Dr. Innsbrook would open a long sermon on horseplay at work. Sure enough, he saw that same "peering through pince-nez" expression settle on her face and opted for diversionary tactics.

"It's my feet, doctor. They've been swollen lately."

The doctor lifted her chin, and Li felt his throat relax.

"Are you going to just stand there growing roots in the floor, or can you haul your butt on the bed where I can examine you?" She looked down at Li's feet. "Sorry, Cinderella, but here you deal with your own shoes."

Li complied, tucking his socks into his shoes and slipping them under the hospital-style bed. He couldn't help looking over his shoulder at the curtain-shrouded corner of the infirmary.

Dr. Innsbrook snapped on a pair of rubber gloves and held Li's foot like an archaeologist inspecting the latest find.

"You had blisters."

Li nodded. "My bunkmate lanced them for me and disinfected my feet."

"Good. That helps. But I can see what you mean by swelling. Does this hurt?" She flexed his foot.

Li cringed.

"On a scale from one to cut my foot off?"

"Seven. Definitely...ow...seven."

"Hmm...Wish we could get a damn X-ray. But then there would be no room if we have to serve as a makeshift morgue."

Li saw his chance, swallowed to moisten his sandpaper throat, and plowed forward. "Yeah...It's still a shock to me. Finding her dead...it just doesn't seem real."

"Yes, well, these things happen."

"Of course, we both know something is wrong about her death, don't we, Doctor?"

Dr. Innsbrook studied the young waiter. Li felt frost collect on his internal organs. "I have no idea what you are talking about, Johnson. And I don't think you do either."

"I think I do." He cast a long glance at the curtains screening a particular bed. His mind went back to the woman, glamorous until her last breath, sunbathing on deck. "Here is a woman whose whole career centered on her appearance—more specifically, on the upkeep of her appearance. A model. A fashion designer. Charlegne Jackson possessed a great deal of pride in how she looked. I think there was also a huge amount of security in it. She was cautious. She kept her physical appearance at the highest possible level. She had to look perfect at all times. Now does that sound like the sort of woman who would forget to apply sunscreen before sunbathing?"

"No. But these things happen." She shed her gloves and washed her hands with quick, brusque movements.

Li swung his bare feet back and forth like a kid on a too-tall chair trying to graze the floor with his toes. "It just doesn't seem likely. And I think something else is bothering you about her death. Something that might explain why Charlegne's eyes were so dilated."

Dr. Innsbrook turned back to her patient, knotted her arms across her chest, and glared. There was molten steel in her eyes.

"Whatever ideas you have churning up there, Johnson, are simply impossible."

"Doctor, I—"

"Impossible, Johnson. I won't say it again."

Li felt all the moisture in his throat evaporate, but stubbornly pressed on. "Doctor, you're an accurate woman. It's part of your work. So when you mention a case that has similarities to one you're working on, accuracy in the details is important to you. They have to match up. Regarding the sunstroke case five years ago, you said the woman passed out from taking too many sleeping pills. Is that what you suspect in Charlegne's death? Is that why her eyes were so dilated?"

Those molten steel eyes whittled into razor-thin slits. "I don't know what sort of after-school, Junior Detective League you grew up in, Johnson, but you are not to utter one syllable about this. Do you understand?" After Li nodded, the medic plopped down next to him. "I can't prove it, but I had a feeling that Charlegne was drugged unconscious when she died. She never knew what the sun did to her. I suspected sleeping pills. Lots of passengers carry them."

Li thought back to the bottle of pills Priscilla knocked over during her melodramatic crying fit. *Charlegne had sleeping pills with her. And I'll never be sure how many were taken from that bottle.*

"Are you sure that—?"

Dr. Innsbrook clipped his question. "No, I can't. I'd like to remind you that we are onboard a luxury cruise ship in the middle of the ocean and do not possess the resources to learn what the specific drug was. All I can be remotely sure of is that Charlegne was drugged and unconscious at the time of her death. Besides, she died from sunstroke, not an overdose. And that's my final opinion on the matter. Now get your shoes on."

Li made the act of donning his socks a slow one. "That makes the coffee all the more interesting."

"I told you I am finished discussing this. Get out."

Li made a ceremony out of tying his shoes. "Because does it make any sense that a woman who took any amount of sleeping pills would then order a cup of black coffee?"

Dr. Innsbrook bounded off the bed and stormed to the sink again. She seized her metal instruments out of the drawers and banged them on the counter. "Stop stalling and get out of my infirmary."

"Why would she order a stimulant after taking a sedative? And why was the cup found on the table to her left?"

"If you don't leave this instant, I'll have the stewards throw you out."

"And something nags at me about the placement of her ring—"

Dr. Innsbrook slammed several tools on the laminate countertop, making a huge, crystalline smash like a falling chandelier. Sudden rushes of red plumed on her face and neck. "What, Johnson? WHAT? Let me guess! It CAN'T have been that stupid bitch who died because that ring on her finger WASN'T the damn ring her fiancé bought her! Is that it? Did I finally hit the goddamn nail on the head?"

Li said nothing. He finished tying his shoes, but he could feel the medic's laser eyes sear into his skull.

Her breathing slowed. The hot bursts of color drained from her cheeks. She froze back into her cool, professional doctor persona. But the molten steel never left her eyes.

"Leave," she said. "It would be as effective to ask you to keep off your feet for a while as it would be to ask one of our passengers to lift a finger. Your examination is done. Go away."

Before Li could even blink, a steward slipped into the infirmary.

"Sorry to interrupt you, Doc, but Captain Crayle asked to see both you and Johnson in his day cabin immediately."

CHAPTER 14

Murder?

"I just learned about a rather unpleasant story working its way around my ship."

Captain Crayle cut an imposing figure behind his desk. His uniform, a loud shock of white against the warm browns of his day cabin, remained crisp and clean as if he had never stepped outside in the elements. His eyes crinkled with laugh lines, but at the moment, they were hard belts of iron-gray.

Dr. Innsbrook sat with her hands folded in her lap. Her back looked like someone welded her spine to rebar. She had all the warmth of an ice carving.

Sweat glazed Li's palms.

Please, God. Don't let it be that stupid sex rumor! Please please PLEASE!

"It seems people are talking about the unfortunate death of Charlegne Jackson," the Captain continued. "I thought I insisted that this tragedy be kept under wraps. Total secrecy. But it seems we have a leak somewhere, don't we? I talked to David Kane and can vouch for him. He's worked on this line long enough to understand discretion. I'd like to give you both an opportunity to speak for yourselves." His eyes softened as he turned to the medic. "Doctor?"

"I never said a word."

Her eyes slanted towards Li. The captain followed suit. Li could see execution written in his steel-hard glare and shrank into his chair.

"I didn't say anything. Honest."

The captain smiled, but it did not soften his gaze. "It's natural, you know, to talk about your day with your friends and coworkers. You might not even realize what you let slip. All I'm saying is that we make mistakes and we need to own up to them."

"I swear, sir, I never told anyone. I swear on my dad's grave."

Captain Crayle allowed one of his eyebrows to rise. "That's an interesting way to put it, son."

"Please, Captain...I promise you that I didn't tell anyone about it. I wouldn't risk my job like that. I'm not stupid."

A soft snort escaped from the doctor.

"It's an admirable defense, but the fact remains, we have a leak. I'd rather plug it now than wait until it explodes. So talk, son. We're your friends here."

The last sentence reminded Li of Aaron Brent.

The young waiter twisted his fingers together. "W-What about the stewards?"

"Stewards?"

"You told David to find two stewards to help him move the body to the infirmary. But they came after you left the deck. So they never heard you telling us to keep it quiet."

"I would expect Kane and Dr. Innsbrook to inform them about my orders."

Li tried to ignore the caustic hatred seeping from the woman seated next to him. "No offense to David or Dr. Innsbrook, but that's kind of like getting an order from a second-in-command. It doesn't carry the same force as when you say it, Captain."

Dr. Innsbrook let her eyes become swords and threatened to impale Li with them.

The captain lifted his hands in mock defeat.

"Anything is possible," he said, "and there really is no reason to keep the secret for much longer."

If there was no reason, Li thought, *why bring me here and scare me half to death?*

Captain Crayle settled back into his chair. "We entered an agreement with Charlegne's lead assistant to stage a memorial on the last day of the cruise. We'll have it in the Horizons Art Gallery, and it will feature Charlegne's clothing designs and modeling shots. I understand Ms. Reilly is spending her day in Ensenada coordinating the whole thing." His eyes, now genuinely laughing, settled on Li. "You'll be quite the hit once people discover that you found the body, son. They'll have a million questions."

Li crumpled in his seat. *You call it a memorial, Captain. I call it a sideshow.*

Dr. Innsbrook seemed to agree with his thoughts. "Isn't that in bad taste, sir? I mean, the woman died in such a horrible, graphic way. Do we really want to exploit that?"

"Tom and Melissa Howard like the idea."

She sniffed disdainfully. "I find that hard to believe, seeing as they hate all publicity."

"Do I sense a personal objection, Dr. Innsbrook?"

She leveled her lecturing face with the captain's, but Li saw how all the color melted out of her skin.

"Doctor?"

The muscles in her forearms tensed. "I have nothing to say."

Li spoke before his brain could slam censors over his mouth. "You mean about how you knew Charlegne personally? Because you did say something about how her ring came from her fiancé. How did you know she even had a fiancé?"

Captain Crayle hardened his gaze on the ship's medic. "Well, doctor?"

"The little snot is lying!"

"I think you better tell us what you know, doctor."

Dr. Innsbrook stiffened and drilled her fury into Li's heart. Although she spoke to the Captain, she never let her hate-heavy glare lift from the boy's face.

"I didn't know her. At least, I never actually met her in person. She knew my ex-husband, Angelo. He ran a clinic in Los Angeles for a while. Probably still runs it. I never really agreed with it. Politics, I expect."

The Captain propped an elbow on the desktop and cradled his chin in his hands. His eyelids drooped. "And when will Charlegne enter this story, doctor?"

"She was Angelo's patient. She came to his clinic over a dozen years ago, I believe. Crying, Angelo said."

"How did you know it was Charlegne?"

"I saw her in the clinic one day when I visited my ex. I recognized her from the cover of *Vogue*. I never spoke to her."

"And how did you know about her fiancé?"

"Angelo mentioned the ring. Said her fiancé must have been flat broke to give her just a speck of a diamond. So when I saw that diamond ring on her finger, I assumed it was her engagement ring. Anyway, it doesn't matter. She was two months along when she came to the clinic. She had the procedure, paid for it, and disappeared." The doctor didn't hide her disgust when she addressed Li. "Well? Does that satisfy your curiosity?"

Li nodded frantically. He could feel a surge of anger pulsing from her.

Captain Crayle drummed his fingers against the wooden desktop, moving so fast that it sounded like an army of horses galloping into war. "There is something strange about this whole thing." He turned to Li again. A nervous tic began to beat in the waiter's jaw. "Why did you bring the ring to Dr. Innsbrook's attention in the first place, son?"

All of Li's insides jammed into his throat, and he choked. "I...um... well..."

"Come clean, boy. Or am I to believe in another interesting story working through my crew?"

Oh God...He knows! He may actually believe Paul! I'm so screwed!

Li found it impossible to swallow. Everything dried up like a scab.

"Talk, boy." The laugh lines around the captain's eyes turned into scowl lines.

"I-It's just that...that some things don't m-make sense about her death, sir."

"What things? Tell me right now."

"Charlegne...Charlegne would have used sunscreen."

"You have no proof."

"Sh-She was a model. Models would take care of their skin. And Charlegne was no fool. I-I don't think it's likely she would have forgotten."

"Immaterial. Moving on."

Sweat bristled on Li's hairline. Now he knew how witnesses felt on cross-examination.

"Her...Her hat."

"Can you get to the point sometime this century?"

"Dr. Innsbrook said that Charlegne didn't w-wear a hat while she died."

"Yes, I saw the burns on her face."

"Well, when I-I found her body, her hat covered her face. I-I'm the one who...who took it off to see who it was."

"Again, immaterial." His eyes said: *Just keep digging that hole, son.*

"Her d-diamond ring—"

"We already went through that. Don't repeat yourself."

"N-No...I meant her ring was on her left hand, and she played with it using her right. She's right-handed."

"So are billions of people."

"But her coffee sat on a table to her left."

"This is getting ridiculous."

"A-And finally there was D-Dr. Innsbrook's latest finding..."

The captain pounced on that one. "Doctor?"

Dr. Innsbrook's expression should have been the cover of a magazine called *If Looks Could Kill.* "She was drugged unconscious when she died. I guessed too many sleeping pills. Maybe something like Rohypnol, but don't quote me on that."

"So are you suggesting, son, that someone drugged Charlegne? Are you saying that Kane put something in her coffee?"

Li shook his head. "No! David didn't do anything to the coffee. I...I tested it. Nothing but black coffee."

"Are you certain of that?"

"I'm still awake, aren't I?"

The ship's medic snorted. "It was clear to me, Captain, that Charlegne simply took too many sleeping pills this morning to catch up on lost sleep, forgot her sunscreen because the pills muddled her thoughts, went to the Sunbathing Deck, and fell asleep. Simple as that."

Captain Crayle flashed a dagger-like smile. "You see, son? It was an accident. It must have been an ugly shock to your system, but nothing sinister happened."

Li wrung his fingers together and focused on a slight scuff on the desktop.

"Unless, of course, you came up with different theory, son..."

It took every reserve of nerves Li had not to quail before the Captain's iron glare.

"I-I think she was murdered."

The captain and the doctor roared with laughter, pounding on the desk with their hands and crying from the sudden pain in their sides.

Rosemary cast a nervous glance at the gilded clock on the nightstand and tried to slip back into the pages of her romance novel. Eleven o'clock already. Where was Martin? He disappeared not long after dinner. He didn't give her a single clue where he went. She struggled to continue reading. Her eyes caught only a few words at a time before flicking up at the door and staring at it. The story was nothing but gibberish now.

She heard voices pass her door—drunk, indistinct. She locked her sights on the doorknob, ready to catch even the tiniest of turns. She didn't really care for Martin when he was drunk, but Martin drunk in her cabin was better than Martin anywhere else.

Oh God...What if he's with—? No, he couldn't be!

A lazy laugh from the passageway seemed to validate all her worst fears. It was feminine, light, slurred on the edges—more of a giggle than a laugh. Her mind taunted her with the image of Charlegne's little titters, the muscles pulling along her neck, and how easy it was to stop the machinery of a human throat.

The drunken murmurs faded. This did nothing to ease her tightly wound nerves. The clock clicked to eleven-oh-two. Rosemary dug her fingernails into the book cover and tried to get interested again in the kidnapping of Geraldine's infant son.

Love Child didn't distract her like she hoped. At times, it was downright painful. Like when Geraldine and Markus met on a bus tour of English gardens and spent the night in their hotel conceiving a beautiful—

Rosemary jerked her head upwards again. Like a cat, she sensed footsteps in the passageway. There were no intoxicated mutterings this time. She felt in her bone marrow that Martin returned to her. It had to be Martin. Martin would never leave her without telling her where he was.

What if he's with her? No, he couldn't be. Marty wouldn't...He couldn't...

She remembered the way his pupils dilated.

Once upon a time, they did that for her.

Lord, please don't let that bitch take Marty away from me!

Rosemary mushed away the sudden tears with the heel of her hand. As such, she missed the nearly imperceptible turn of the doorknob. The door inched open. Martin Hale slid into the cabin.

"Marty...Oh Marty! I've just been insane with—"

She stopped. She inspected her husband. He wasn't drunk, but his smooth, slightly sunburned face looked thirty years older than it should have.

"Marty, dear...What—?"

"Rosie...I have something to tell you."

It came. It finally came. She was shocked that her immediate impulse was sadness, not fury. Anger came easily to her. She had no explanation to why she reacted with mute terror, replaying the audio loop of her husband's planned announcement in her thrashing brain. He loved Charlegne. He would divorce Rosemary. She wondered how it would feel to suffer irreparable damage to her still broken heart. He loved Charlegne—

No! He didn't say "We need to talk!" That's what all the bastards say when they're going to ruin your life! He didn't say anything yet! He didn't say "We need to talk," so it can't be that bad! Don't break the rules, Marty!

"What is it, honey?"

"I...I went down to the infirmary..."

All her feminine alarms flared. Doctors were bad. Rosemary hated them. She and her husband planned to use this cruise as an escape from doctors and hospitals and one depressing diagnosis. So far, it had been a failure from conception.

Conception—that was the worst word she could have chosen.

"W-Why?"

It couldn't have been the same diagnosis as hers, the one where her gynecologist said it was physically impossible for her to conceive a child.

Rosemary had cried through the whole spring season after that.

"Rosie...Charlegne's dead."

No reaction. Not even a slight gasp.

Then *Love Child* tumbled out of her hands and onto the floor.

"You have to admit that it's pretty hard to believe, Li," Travis said while he closed up the Temptations bar. "And I thought we weren't talking to each other? Or does that rule always break at midnight, Cinderella?"

"I wanted to show you that I wasn't lying before." Li crossed his arms and directed a stony glare at his friend. "Your imagination worries me."

"I don't think I'm the one with the wild imagination."

"I know it sounds a little crazy, but—"

"Oh, it sounds more than just a little crazy, Li. I mean, how can anyone murder Charlegne Jackson with sunstroke?" Travis tossed a rag at his friend's face. "Sorry to be the evil stepbrother, Cinderella, but I need you to help me wipe down the tables in the lounge."

"How come?"

"Aw, come on, Li. Just do this for me."

"If I'm going to survive a night of Cinderella cracks, I'd like to know why I have to help you clean."

"Oh, fine. I'm just in a rotten mood." He began scrubbing his bottled-up anger into the first tabletop. "Mr. Brent the Bastard kicked up one of his famous fits about all the tables being—let me see if I can get all his words in—'scuffed, dingy, tasteless pieces of bloated donkey crap.' Sprinkle in some random swear words and add a hiccup or two and you get the idea. Anyway, his complaints wouldn't stop until the bosses gave the orders for me to scrub down every last table at closing."

"Just the tops?"

"Tops and bases. He's a thorough son of a bitch."

"And how clean are we supposed to make these spotless pieces of art?"

Travis grinned at Li's sarcasm. "Until the only stain is Mr. Brent's reflection when he looks at them. Let's hope these babies don't collapse in terror when he does."

Li glanced at the sheen of the thirty-odd black laminate tabletops and the sparkle of the chrome bases. He groaned at the wasted effort.

"This makes me wonder what on Earth his job could be. I can't think of anyone who'd want to hire him."

"He's a corporate attorney. His clientele includes some of the biggest scum-sucking bastards of our time. He gloated about them sometime between his second and third bottle of Scotch."

"A corporate attorney...I guess that makes sense. He does love to argue."

"Arguing is just a euphemism for what he does. And scum can always recognize one of their own." Travis squatted and scrubbed the mirror finish of one of the bases, as if trying to buff out his own reflection. "It's just like crazies on the street. They seem to flock together. Maybe you can join them, Li, with this brilliant murder theory of yours."

Li whacked his friend on the butt with his rag.

"Hey! If you just wanted to come onto me—!"

110

"Don't flatter yourself, Travis. That's what you get for calling me crazy. And for whipping me with your towel every chance you get."

"I guess I deserve that. But come on, Li! You have to admit this whole Charlegne plus murder thing sounds like something a person would scrawl on a loony bin bathroom wall. It's just impossible!"

"Tricky yes, but not impossible."

"Are you going to abuse me and my drowsiness by giving me some long, complicated lecture a la Dr. Innsbrook?"

"Keep this up and I might."

"That is probably the nastiest threat you have ever made to me. But go on and tell me your genius theory already. Why do you think someone murdered Charlegne?"

Li repeated—this time without stammering—the conversation he had with the doctor and captain.

Travis stopped polishing his umpteenth table. "So all you have is a list of negligent behavior on Charlegne's part? And somehow this equals an evil mastermind with a flair for accidents?"

Li felt his confidence slip a notch. "Well, it's just that—"

"I think someone else stayed in the sun too long. Dial back on your imagination, Li."

"I didn't make any of it up!"

"I don't recall suggesting that." Travis counted off the remaining tables on his fingers. "Look, buddy, I never said you invented all this stuff, but I think you strung it all together in your hyperactive imagination and created a plot that isn't there. You had an ugly shock. Finding a body on the anniversary of your father's nasty death is enough to unravel anyone. After a good night of total unconsciousness, you'll see that everything you thought is just ridiculous. I'm sorry."

Li examined his reflection in the chrome base he buffed. Hard wrinkles of exhaustion dug into his skin. Could he really have imagined all this nonsense after all? The ring of his slack, tired mouth reminded him of the golden band and its molecule of a diamond on Charlegne's hand.

"Someone moved the body."

Travis's head bobbed up over a tabletop. "What was that, Li?"

"Someone moved Charlegne's body."

"Oh yeah? Where's your proof?"

"She sat in the wrong chair. David knew Charlegne's habits and would have set the coffee to her right, because she was right-handed. But when we found her, the coffee sat on her left. There's only one answer: Someone moved her body one seat to the right. Dr. Innsbrook thinks Charlegne took several sleeping pills this morning and fell asleep. She would never notice the move."

"Why would someone move her?"

"I...I don't know."

A smug curl twisted Travis's lips. "I have a smarter answer."

"Oh, I can't wait to hear this."

"Charlegne moved herself." He cut off Li's protest. "You know I'm right. She got up herself and left the deck to do something. Maybe take a shower, which is why there was no sunscreen on her skin. She felt tired, so she took a few pills. She went back on deck. Unfortunately, the drug muddled her brain, and she left her bottle of sunscreen in her cabin. She sat in the wrong chair, which is an easy mistake since all the chairs share tables and the pills confused her. See? Pure accident."

"Sorry, Perry Mason, but there's a hole in your theory."

Travis stood, balled up his rag, threw it on the table, and locked his hands on his hips. "Oh yeah, smarty? Lay it on me! I'll plug it up cleaner than you ever could."

"You said Charlegne simply left the sunscreen in her cabin. But I went to her stateroom today. There was no bottle of sunscreen anywhere. Her assistant even worried about misplacing a bottle that Charlegne 'never sunbathed without,' and I have a suspicion that it was sunscreen. It just disappeared."

"Ha! That's all you have? I can putty that up no problem. I'll change my theory a little. Charlegne did take sunscreen with her, just like you said a former model would do. She falls asleep from the pills, and someone comes along and throws the bottle into the sea."

Li tossed his own rag on the table he just cleaned. "So you agree it's a murder!"

"Oh shut up, Li. It was probably a dumb prank. It didn't kill her. The sun did. You can't murder someone with the sun."

"I think someone could."

"Oh, I can't wait to hear this theory. It'll be the best sleep aid I'll ever have."

Li restrained his temper. "Look, if we can accept the fact that you can die from sunstroke, we should be able, without too much fantasy..." Travis smirked at that. "...to accept that someone can murder with sunstroke. It's as simple as abandoning someone in a sunny location without any protection. The sun will affect them."

"So?"

"So taking away a bottle of sunscreen is definitely taking away protection."

"Again, this is just a theory. I still say it was a stupid prank."

"But who would prank her like that?"

Travis picked up his rag and twisted it. "Definitely not one of the crew. That would mean immediate firing. None of us can live without this gig. So it had to be a passenger."

Li pulled his sleepy face into a grimace. "I really hate to admit it, Travis, but I think you might be right about that."

"Say it again, buddy. I don't think you sounded quite reluctant enough."

"Okay, fine. You win. A passenger came along and stole Charlegne's sunscreen."

His brain added: *But I still feel like it's a murder.*

"Well, thank you, Li. I'm positively bubbling with repressed joy right now. I would probably float to the ceiling if my shoes didn't weigh several tons. Let's do these last six tables before I start snoring."

They concluded the cleanup, locked the lounge, and prepared to pass out in their bunks.

"You know that guy you saw in the restaurant on the island," Li asked as they bundled into the elevator.

"Short Fuse or Chain Smoker?"

"The smoker. What did he look like?"

Travis crinkled up his face with the rigors of memory. "Um...balding... dark hair, graying at the temples...sweats a lot...wears a suit that costs more than a neighborhood in L.A...shiny shoes that Paulie would drool over. Why?"

Li's own memory awoke. "Doesn't he work with Charlegne? I've seen them together."

"I think the proper preposition you want is 'for.' They were all her servants. They worked for her. No one worked with her."

"Grammar aside, who is he?"

"He's Steven something. He's Charlegne's business manager."

Li sewed his eyebrows together in a taut frown.

Her business manager?

CHAPTER 15

Witnesses

Crap crap crap crap CRAP!

Li overslept. The strain of yesterday had knocked him unconscious as soon as he plopped on his mattress. When his eyes finally pried open, it was ten to seven. Li vaulted out of bed, tripped over his shoes, limped to the bathroom, tumbled into his clothes, and threw himself out of his quarters with his shirt untucked and a terminal case of bedhead. He didn't care if he looked bad. If he was late to work, Paul would add to the ugly bruises ballooning across his face. Then fire him. It was enough to make the good eye wince.

Of all the days to be late for work! I might as well throw myself off the ship and save Paul the trouble!

Li bolted out of the elevator, hoping to squeak into the dining room before too many passengers settled for breakfast. He caught a glimpse of the scarlet neon letters advertising Temptations. A lopsided grin of triumph brightened his face. Almost there. He was literally a heartbeat away. He would slink into the dining room with all the liquid agility of a cat.

He should have remembered his rotten luck.

Daphne Cole, her relentless voice rising even under the puzzle of purses, carry-ons, and camera bags she carried, bustled towards the dining room. Every trace of Li's feline dexterity deserted him, and the two collided. Li heard something rip and thought a torn work shirt at this stage would be just the right epitaph in the tombstone of his cruise line career.

"I'm so sorry, ma'am! Here let me help you up."

"Oh, it's okay! Not a scratch! I wasn't paying attention where I was going. You're not hurt, are you?" She straightened her blouse and inspected his face. "Oh! You're the adorable waiter who served us yesterday!"

Li felt his cheeks prickle with heat. He didn't feel particularly "adorable" with a shiner darkening and swelling around one eye like an eye patch.

"Um...right...that's me." The memory of the cold, steel gleam of hate in her husband's drill bit eyes made Li cramp with fear. "Let me help you, ma'am."

"You're so sweet! Most young men would just run off and let me deal with it. Isn't that just disgusting?"

"Yes, it's horrible, Mrs.—?"

"Cole. Daphne Cole." She collected her things from Li and let out a soft moan. She lifted an issue of *Vogue* magazine, a ragged tear splitting a model's face on the front cover. "Oh rats! I hoped to have Charlegne sign this while I was here."

"Charlegne?"

Daphne let loose a whole orchestra of squeals and giggles, making enough noise for three women and dropping several of her returned carry-ons on the floor again. Li feared for his eardrums. "Oh yes! I had the most thrilling encounter yesterday morning! Oh, I wish I could tell Linda and Marcia about it! They'd simply keel over with jealousy!"

Li wondered, as he stooped to pick up the newly scattered belongings, whether some women survived through never-ending cycles of one-upmanship with their closest friends.

Daphne shadowed him, determined to pummel the young waiter with her story. "Of course, they were already RIDDLED with envy when I told them about Josh's sister giving us this cruise as a gift. But things have been hard at home lately, and I thought we deserved this vacation. And what a vacation it's been! Such a nice staff! I told that man yesterday that the employees really look after us like—now what was that rather clever phrase I used?—'shepherds with their flock.' I grew up around farms, so the associations are always there."

Li felt pins of anxiety around his mouth as he counted the seconds. It wasn't that Mrs. Cole was a bad person, but her penchant for salting her stories with anecdotes eroded a person's patience after a while.

"This cruise has been like a fairytale for Josh and me! It's just been unbelievable!"

The young waiter restored the twice-fallen jumble of purses to their owner and turned toward the dining room, hoping he had enough seconds to start waiting a table before Paul clued in on his tardiness.

"Of course, I couldn't believe my luck when I saw Charlegne Jackson that morning!"

It was a second or two of mental hell as Li wrestled between duty and curiosity.

Despite his common sense screaming and pulling at his hair to keep him from turning back, he faced Daphne again. "You saw Charlegne Jackson?"

Daphne seemed to purr at the idea of finally securing a rapt audience. "Well, you see, at breakfast yesterday, I rescued this very sweet woman named Sally from her boar of a husband. Dear Josh helped me out. He knows how to negotiate with…difficult clients. He talked to Sally's husband. We simply had to get Sally away for a while. Poor thing. She must have been bullied by men all her life. Well anyway, she and I made plans to meet on the Seaview Deck at ten and go to Catalina Island. I went there early, because Josh said he needed to talk to someone."

"You didn't go to the island with your husband?"

"Well, we planned to go on the Airport-in-the-Sky tour, but I thought it would be best if Sally had a girl's day. Just the two of us. I never left Sally alone for a moment. I didn't want her to think I'd abandon her or anything like that. I made sure she always knew I was there for her. We girls have to stick together like glue. Besides, my husband could enjoy himself on his own. He went to the Airport while I took Sally to the Casino. You know it has these gorgeous murals."

I'm going to be here until dinner service at this rate, Li thought. He started inching backwards.

Daphne edged closer to Li. "It was just spectacular! I thought I would burn through my entire media card on the murals alone! Luckily, I brought spares. Oh, and we met this lovely woman down on Deck Three while we waited for the tenders! Priscilla's her name."

Priscilla? Could it be the same Priscilla as Charlegne's assistant?

"It was like being with the girls again. Priscilla joined Sally and me on our tour. She took us to this fabulous dress shop on the island and helped me pick this drop dead gorgeous gown of blue...was it silk? I can't recall. Anyway, it was a delightful store, and Priscilla's expert tips really helped us decide what clothes would be best for our figures. We would have stayed longer, but Sally had a headache and wanted to stop at a drug store for some aspirin. So we did. I even offered to pay for it."

"How nice of you." Li craned his neck over his shoulder as he heard polite, breakfast chatter waft from the dining room mere centimeters away. If he could beg Daphne off...but a new thought flared to life like a filament zapped with electric current. "This lady, Priscilla, had expert fashion tips?"

"Oh yes! Didn't I say why? Sometimes I get so wrapped up in my stories. She works for Charlegne Jackson at *La Charlegne.*" Daphne started twittering and fluttering like a startled bird, and Li was terrified that she would drop her belongings again. "Oh, just listen to me! I didn't even get to tell you about that morning with Charlegne! I always seem to run off on a tangent. There was one time when I...No, no...I need to tell you about Charlegne. I was more thrilled than I have ever been in my life!"

Li's feet continued to slink backwards even as his ears honed in on the words spewing over Daphne's lips. "I bet you were, Mrs. Cole."

Just another inch or two. If I can get her into the dining room, then it won't look so bad. I won't seem so late. Oh God, I hope so.

"Well, like I said, I went to the Sports Deck at about five to ten to wait for Sally. We were meeting at that little strip of deck covered by the awning...the Seaview Deck. This nice attendant came to me and said I would be more comfortable waiting by the pool, because it was not as chilly. It was pretty nippy on the Seaview Deck, so I went and sat next to this man already there. Quiet guy. Didn't say anything to me. Well, I talked for a minute or two and then—this is the best part—I saw Charlegne Jackson herself come up from the lower decks! Oh, it was priceless. Like looking through a magazine all over again. She wore this delicious white bathing suit. A one-piece with little cutouts in the side. Modest and yet, cut to fit her figure in the most flattering way. And she perched this chic purple sunhat on her head. She sauntered along like it was a boulevard in Paris. Gliding almost. She even waved to me! Can you imagine? I could have fainted dead away when that happened!"

"I can imagine, yes. What did Charlegne do?"

Daphne waved away her idol's actions with a slight sigh. "Oh, nothing special. She just sat in a lounge chair and ordered coffee. Then tipped the hat over her eyes and fell asleep. It was a perfect day to sunbathe."

So Charlegne covered her face with the hat. But someone had to take it off for the sun to affect her brain and then put it back on later. Why? And did she use sunscreen?

"Of course, the minute I saw her, I said 'I need to get her autograph.' I always take an issue of *Vogue* when I travel. I thought 'I'll ask her to sign this.' It would be so poetic! Well, wouldn't you know it? The moment I decide to do that, it turns out I left my purse and my magazine in my cabin! I tore down to my cabin, hoping I could make it in time to meet Sally. It wasn't easy. There was this mass of people trying to leave the ship the second the tenders did, and it was like plowing upstream all the way. It took me ages to reach the Seaview Deck again. Sally was there. I hoped I didn't keep her waiting too long. We left right after that, because we had so much to do."

"But what about your autograph?"

"Silly me. I left the magazine in the stateroom again. I just grabbed my purse and left." She sighed indulgently. "Oh, I do hope I get to meet Charlegne Jackson in person! I'm simply dying to tell Linda and—Oh hello, Honeybunch! I've missed you."

Li ran his back right into another person and stuttered to a stop. He pivoted his head upwards. The angry, dark eyes of Josh Cole glared down at him. They were like coals starting to smolder. His red hair blazed under the cold white light pouring in from the Atrium.

Short Fuse, Li thought. *This must be Short Fuse.*

"I was just grabbing some more stuff for when we depart the ship, and I ran into this sweet boy. Do you remember him from yesterday?"

Josh clapped two hard hands onto the waiter's shoulders. Li flinched. Then he felt those hungry, tendon-tight paws inch around his throat.

"Oh, I remember all right."

Li found it hard to swallow.

"Come on, Daphne dear. Let's have breakfast."

"Just think, Joshy-poo! We're in Ensenada, Mexico! Oh, it's so exotic!"

"It'll be an adventure, my angel."

Giving the throat a warning squeeze, Josh shoved Li out of his way and escorted his wife into the dining room. Li crashed into the wall. Fearing a banged-up shoulder in the midst of all his other problems, he watched the receding couple and grazed his fingertips along his neck

Daphne Cole glanced over her shoulder and waved airily at him. She smiled without strain, untroubled by her husband's behavior.

Li wondered if a woman's friendliness might mean murder to her friends.

"Hey buddy! You and I need to settle something."

Travis slipped into the kitchen just as Li finished washing the dishes. His eyes scanned the rows of china, silverware, and cookware lined in the drying racks like an army. He let out a long whistle. "First of all, are you still on solo dish duty?"

Li racked the last clean plate with its brothers and dried his hands on a dish towel. "Well, ever since Paul's edict, the dishwashers made themselves scarce. This is a vacation for them."

"They might want to take a permanent one. I've never seen it so organized."

Li twisted his towel and blushed. "I like it that way. Keeps everything where it's supposed to be. My brain hates chaos. I don't mind the job so much now. Gives me a chance to get away from people for a while."

"Speaking of getting away, are you going on the crew excursion this time or not? Don't give me your usual, half-assed excuses, Li, because—"

"Of course, I'm going."

"—if you go on about being in 'mourning,' I'll—wait...what did you say?"

"I said I'm going, Travis. I decided last night. There's no way I'm staying on this ship for another round of abuse."

"It would be less abusive today since Paulie and the sommelier always go on the wine tasting tour in Guadalupe together to schmooze our liquor-loving luminaries."

Li hooked his dish rag on the drying rack. "Really? Then maybe I should change my mind and stay."

"Don't you dare! I already have your word. We're going to the sea geyser, La Bufadora or 'The Blowhole.' You can guess why I'm interested." He waggled his eyebrows. "So hurry up and get changed into something more casual and fun and less like you're serving me a tray of daiquiris. Although that wouldn't be a bad idea, eh buddy?" He elbowed Li in the ribs. "I'll meet you in front of the welcome center. It's right on the pier. Can't miss it. Don't take forever, okay?"

"I won't, Travis. The only thing keeping me here is you." Li grinned. "So get lost already!"

"Now that's what I call friendship." Travis winked, turned to the swinging kitchen doors, hesitated, and then doubled back. "I better leave the back way. I heard this couple behind me when I came in, and it sounded like they wanted to use the empty dining room as their private fight club. Don't want to walk in on that. That's your job."

"Are you saying that I'm the one who has to ask them to leave?"

"Would there be anyone better?"

Travis saluted his friend as the service elevator doors closed around him. Li pushed out a sigh, tried to remember the scraps he learned taking karate as a kid, just in case, and parted the kitchen doors a crack.

Rosemary spoke to a sandy-haired man who had his back to Li. Both were dressed in loose summer clothes, ready for a relaxing tour of Ensenada. Something was off. Li could see the tightly suppressed tension in Rosemary's face. Her hair was an unbound eruption of ginger curls. Her chin thrust forward. Jungle green eyes flashed like the scales of a dragon.

His common sense, now sounding more like his mother, wailed at him to follow Travis's lead, but Li chose to listen.

"I don't understand this protest, Martin. Why shouldn't I be allowed to enjoy my vacation?"

"Rosie, darling, do you always have to fight with me?"

"Maybe. Maybe it's become the fun part of our marriage."

"Charlegne just died, Rosie. Do you have to look like you just won the lottery? People will talk."

"Do you think I've spent my whole life worrying about what people think?"

"Rosie..."

The man named Martin cupped his wife's face with his hand. Rosemary's gaze lowered to the floor.

"The sweetheart trick won't work, Martin. Not this time."

"Dear, you're not even trying to listen to—"

"Maybe I don't want to listen." Her chin shot back up, and there was a challenge in her eyes. "Ever think of that, darling? Either way, none of it matters. The bitch is dead. My life doesn't have to end just because hers did."

"And yet, when she was alive, you let her run your life. You would throw everything away just to stay away from her."

"That's different. When she lived, she made me remember Dustin. Now that she's gone, I don't have to worry about those damn memories. When she died, they died." Rosemary attempted a bored shrug, but her shoulders were too tense. "I think it's better this way."

Martin took her hand. His voice softened. "Even after fifteen years?"

"Fifteen years means nothing. At least, I'VE tried to move on. I'M not worried about her anymore, eh Martin? She's dead. There's no more... temptation." She lifted the corners of her mouth into a smile, but the smile didn't touch her sharp, narrow glare. "You know all about that, don't you my dear, devoted husband?"

Li could sense that the dragon she chained in her heart was about to escape. He shrank further into the kitchen.

"I...I have no idea what you mean, Ro—"

"Don't you, sweetie? Don't you think I pay attention to my husband's behavior?" Martin cringed. "Don't you think I'd be curious about my husband's reactions to certain things?" Her nostrils flared, her pupils clenched into the slits of a snake, and Li saw her features mutate into the dragon's face. "Don't you think, after twenty-two years, I would know when my husband wanted to screw another woman?"

Li's heart came to a full stop. He remembered Charlegne in the dining room doorway again. How the ice she built around her shattered. How she seemed to melt into a different woman. How even he felt hot and bothered when he saw the real woman under all the glamour.

Li knew the woman Rosemary meant.

Rosemary slid her hand out of her husband's grip. Bright wheels of color flushed her cheeks. She swung her sunglasses down onto the bridge of her nose like the blade of a guillotine. It was a gesture reminiscent of Charlegne.

"You stay here and wait for me, Marty dear. I need a few minutes by myself. I'll come back soon, and we'll get on the tour." She leaned in and kissed his cheek. That seemed to wound her husband more than her words. "I love you, Marty. Remember that. I'M the one who loves you."

She sailed out of the dining room.

Li shuffled out of the kitchen. He cleared his desert of a throat.

Martin wheeled around at the noise. Fear sparked in his chestnut eyes before settling into a searching, calculating glare. He fished out his checkbook.

"How much do you want, kid?"

Li's eyebrows inched upwards. "I'm not interested in—"

"I know you overheard my wife and me. And I won't have you breathing a word of this to anyone. So how much do you want?" He clicked a ball-point pen against his leg. It sounded like cocking the hammer on a pistol.

"I don't want your money."

"What do you want?"

"To tell you the dining room is closed, Mr. Hale."

"I have to wait here for my wife. And how do you know my name?"

Li swallowed and refused to make eye contact.

"Wait...I know you. You were our waiter. Rosie has some kind of crush on you. Thinks you're sweet. But there's this nasty rumor I heard from one of your coworkers...and if you even think about sleeping with my wife, I'll—"

"I'd never sleep with your wife! And I didn't sleep with Charlegne!"

"That's what you claim. I think you'd better stick to serving customers in the dining room only." Martin turned and strode toward the door.

"You loved Charlegne, didn't you?" Li called out after him.

Martin stopped. He looked over his shoulder, and there was solid hate in his eyes. Then he ambled toward Li, each step measured, controlled. Li suppressed the instinct to flee.

"I love Rosie. It's as simple as that. I can't dream of living with anyone but her." His tone was as measured as his footsteps.

"But you still wanted Charlegne?"

"Who says that?"

"It seems every man found her attractive."

"Ha! Attractive?" Martin spat, "It was lust! Pure, stupid lust! I can't think of a man on this planet who didn't moan to her at some point during puberty!" He stopped walking and unbuttoned the collar of his Hawaiian print shirt. His cheeks flamed. "Can you imagine the hell I live in? To want to screw the damn daylights out of the woman your wife loathes? There were times when I hurt myself trying to release the tension."

"I...I understand."

Martin smirked. "Dumb statement, kid. Anyone with a Y chromosome craved that bitch. And she never wanted anyone. Not after..." He trailed off.

"But you saw her yesterday while you waited for the tenders, right?"

Martin's hand lunged at Li's throat. It cut off the shout Li might have made.

"Say a word of this to my wife and I'll crush you. Do you understand me?" He shook Li by the throat, making the head flop in a lazy nod. "I didn't touch that bitch. I have witnesses who will vouch for me. The deck attendant. Some woman who couldn't shut up."

He let go of the wheezing boy.

Li choked on his words. "B-But you saw h-her."

"You want to hear the story? Fine. After breakfast, Rosie and I went to our cabin. She said she didn't feel well and wanted to rest before going ashore. I went on the Sports Deck at about nine-fifty to wait for her. The deck attendant pulled out a chair by the pool, and I sat there."

Li's engine of a brain whirred into life. *And yet, only a few minutes later, Rosemary went on deck herself, but avoided her husband. Why?*

"I fantasized about Charlegne. It hurt, but what could I do? The little witch got into my system. I've been trying to sweat her out for years. At five to ten, this irritating woman came on deck, talking nonstop about how 'amazing' her trip was. She's one of those women who has to hear the sound of her voice at all times. I could have socked the attendant for seating her next to me. I really didn't need her inane chatter."

"And Charlegne?"

"She came up just a minute or two before ten. About gave me a heart attack. That chatty woman wouldn't shut up about Charlegne. Who knows? When she learns her idol is dead, she might actually stop talking."

"How did you know about Charlegne's death?"

Martin's eyes narrowed. "Why should you care? I didn't do anything wrong. I heard some stewards talk about it, so I went down to the infirmary. Figured that's where they'd hide her. When I was there, I heard voices." Sandy eyebrows jumped up his forehead. "It was you! You talked about it! I recognize your voice! How did you know about it?"

Li crossed his arms to smother the shakes in his fingers. "I found her body."

"So is that what this is? Morbid curiosity?"

CHAPTER 16

Mexico

So this is Mexico...

Li stepped onto the asphalt peninsula serving as the pier and cast his sights on the sail-sized Mexican flag shadowing the Bahía de Todos Santos. Like the Statue of Liberty, it welcomed strangers to its home. He made it. He was in the Port of Ensenada on the Gold Coast of Baja California, his first time out of the country. Li wondered what his dad would think of this bustling spot with the sun shining with the arrogance of a Hollywood legend and the turquoise tint to the harbor.

But he also wondered what his dad would think about the purple bruise bleeding across his pale skin.

Travis hailed his friend from across the pier, standing before a lurid, burnt-red building designed to look like a Spanish mission, although the paint scheme revealed it was too new to be authentic. Tourists swamped the place, jabbering and posing for pictures. Li, glad for the well-broken sneakers on his feet, hurried to his friend.

"You made it!" Travis said. "I was starting to wonder whether you would flake on me. I don't like being stood up."

"Almost as much as you hate being cooped up." Li cupped his hands around his eyes and peered into the welcome center. Stalls crowded the open room, selling wares from jewelry to leather goods to liquor. Tourists, mostly female, flitted from booth to booth like bees. Their husbands and boyfriends babysat the growing mounds of shopping bags from benches in the middle of the building.

"You can go inside, Li. We're allowed to be normal people out here."

Li's smile brightened his face and smoothed out all his stress lines. "I wish we could actually get something. I don't have much cash on me, but..."

Travis chuckled at his friend's transparent enthusiasm. "Nothing wrong with a little window shopping. Maybe you'll get lucky. Besides, we have time to kill before—Whoa!"

Li wrenched his eyes from the welcome center, and his jaw went slack. Travis had the same, open-mouthed look of astonishment on his face.

A woman paraded across the asphalt with Steven Danforth trailing behind her. She wore a tightly cinched cream peplum suit jacket and a black, knee-length pencil skirt. Her stiletto heels clicked like horseshoes across the ground. Black gloves sheathed her hands, her fingers crusted with rings. She crowned the look with a large hat, black and cream and better suited for the Kentucky Derby than a trip to Mexico.

The wide hat brim tilted up, and Li thought his jaw would scrape against the asphalt.

It was Priscilla Reilly. She made a transformation that could rival butterflies.

"Close your mouths, boys," she said. Her silvery laugh echoed in Li's ears as she marched into the welcome center. Steven's upper lip curled in disgust, but he followed.

Travis whistled and rubbed his eyes. "You must have kept me waiting out in the sun too long, Li. Did I just see Ms. Dowdy-Dear Reilly stroll up here looking like an evil Charlegne Jackson clone?"

Li tried to bring moisture back to his throat. "Uh-huh."

"Now I'm sorry I didn't believe your murder theory, buddy."

"What does that have to do with Ms. Reilly changing her clothes?"

"Because if anyone is going to kill Charlegne..." He gestured to the door. "...it would be our newly-crowned Princess Priscilla. She got her claws into the label before Charlegne's body went cold. I bet she's been waiting for years."

Li closed his eyes and massaged his right temple. *I should have known,* he thought. *Priscilla's a social climber. Shrewd. Manipulative. Opportunistic. She attached herself to a luxury label, created this frumpy, emotional character, gained Charlegne's trust, and, when the impossible happened, took control of the whole business. A slick plan. How far would she go?*

"Makes me wonder how long she had those clothes stashed away," Travis said, breaking Li's thoughts.

"Years probably." *She used fashion to emphasize her character. Sagging, oversized blouses and dresses in off-putting colors to establish this submissive personality and, when Charlegne died, a nun-like dress thing to stress her 'emotional suffering.' There were times when she slipped. Sometimes she over-acted the part. Sometimes the shrewd mind broke through, like when she gave expert fashion tips. Now she can revert to normal Priscilla. Her plan succeeded.*

Travis shook his head in disbelief. "I don't think she can pull it off. Charlegne was the line. The only reason it existed is because of her energy, or something. She knew how to make people do what she wanted."

A head poked out of the welcome center. "Are you ladies going to keep talking about fashion, or can we get on this tour?"

"David?" Li asked. "Are you coming too?"

David sidled out of the building. He gave Li a very military salute, but a grin rich with teeth lit up his face. "Your tour guide at your service, sir."

"I thought that since this is your first time in Mexico," Travis said, "you should have a quality tour guide. David's been on this route more than anyone else. So I asked him to come. Sound okay to you, Li?"

Li rolled his eyes. "Does Paul over-wax his shoes?"

"Again with fashion. Can't you talk about manlier things?" David checked his watch. "Whoa! No time for that. We're going to be late. They arranged an earlier tour for the Howard Line crew, so let's get a move on."

"Good idea. Besides, I want to get back in time to have dinner in the crew mess."

"You're in a foreign country, Li, and you still want dinner on the ship?"

Li folded his arms across his chest. "Chef Jack is making his grandfather's fried chicken. I don't care what you say. Neither of you will deny me my one guilty pleasure. I think I've earned it."

"*La Cenicienta del Pacífico,*" David said, the Spanish rolling sensuously off his tongue. "That's what the port-dwellers—the *porteños*—call their city. The Cinderella of the Pacific. Heart of Mexican wine country. Cosmopolitan center on the make. Rags to riches. You can relate, huh Li?"

Li pulled his gaze from the jostled view out the bus window and frowned at his bunkmate. "You're the third person to compare me with Cinderella. What gives?"

"Well, you don't have a lot of money or status, and you're pretty much a slave on the ship..."

Travis leaned across the aisle separating their seats. "And you have issues with shoes and curfews."

Li rolled his eyes and returned to the view. "Why does it look like some of these buildings are unfinished?"

"You noticed that?" David asked, quirking an eyebrow.

"My dad was a contractor. I know what a finished product looks like."

"Well, you see..." David's voice dropped to a conspiratorial level. "...there's a law here that states when a building is completed, property tax goes into effect. So..." He left the rest to Li's imagination.

Urban sprawl melted into farmland. Li devoured David's stories like a kindergartner on his first field trip. His smile was irrepressible. He looked alarmingly young, his skin smooth, untroubled, and flushed with eagerness. Even his bruises seemed to fade. He laughed freely, told a few jokes his dad used to tell, and drank in the atmosphere of having escaped his grief.

David and Travis studied him with mirrored expressions of curiosity and suspicion.

"First time out of the country?" David asked.

Li wiped away the tears brewing from the latest laughing fit. "Yep. My family didn't have much money to travel. I thought you knew that."

"I did. It's just you look really young."

Li's brow puckered, and he threw a sidelong glance at his bunkmate. "Well, I'm only twenty."

Travis came to David's rescue. "He means you look like your age again. Usually your face has so many stress lines, a steam iron would be intimidated. Now you're laughing and smiling, looking like a kid again. Eighteen at most."

"Like the little brother I never had," David embellished.

"You try to act mature and let all the crap roll off your back, but it doesn't really work." Li's forehead creased with a frown. "Sorry, buddy. We can see right through you. You're a broke, homesick kid still grieving for your dad and terrified of the future. Didn't Cinderella—?"

"Oh, for God's sake, Travis!" Li snapped. "Not again!"

"Wait a second," said David. "If Li's Cinderella, who's the Fairy Godmother?"

"Hey, are you seriously going to talk as if I'm not here?"

"Maybe his Fairy Godmother hasn't shown up yet." Travis craned his head to look at his scowling friend over David's shoulder. "Hear that, Li? You still have a chance to go to the ball!" He snickered.

"You ignored me just to irritate me, right?"

"Duh!" David and Travis matched grins and fist-bumped.

Li's ears burned red. "I hate you both."

"And we take security in the knowledge that you will never seek vengeance," David replied.

Li's eyes widened. A little lightning bolt of a thought flashed in his head. He awarded his attention to the view again, watching as the green furrows of farmland hardened into the rocky crags of the shoreline. "Security," he muttered to himself. "Why didn't you call?"

"What was that, Li?" David asked.

Li turned away from the window. "When the passenger held those stewards hostage yesterday, why didn't you call security, David? There's a phone right next to the beverage station."

"Don't you think I know that? I did call. Twice. Couldn't get through."

"But there's always someone manning the security desk."

"I'm not the guy who decides when they take their coffee breaks, Li. I called security shortly after I learned we had hostages. No answer. I tried to calm the woman down, nearly had my head popped off by one of her paws, and tried again. Still no answer. That's when I tried the whiskey and soda. That seemed to work the best."

"That doesn't make any sense, though." Li slipped into his thoughts. *Someone should have taken that call. If security missed something like that, who's to say they didn't miss anything that happened to Charlegne on deck? But the cameras...Wait! The cameras! That's it!*

David shrugged. "I'm not here to make sense of what people do. I'm just here to show you around, Li."

Travis stretched and yawned like a cat ready to shift his position in the sun. "I'm here for the tequila. Are we there yet?"

"Keep your shirt on, Patrelli. When it feels like the bus is trying to throw you out of your seat, we're in the parking lot."

In fifteen minutes, the bus bumped and bounced over the half-buried boulders in the dirt parking lot. Li thanked several supreme deities for insisting he have a lighter breakfast, given the stomach acrobatics the bus gave him. Once parked, the tourists lurched out of their coach, undid a few kinks in their joints, and strolled towards the market.

"So where's this geyser, Dave-o?" Travis asked, stretching a knot out of his back. "This looks more like the marketplace in *Aladdin*. You didn't kidnap us to go shopping, did you?"

"It's at the end of the market." David waved a hand down the dirt path curling like a snake through the column of shops and stalls. "There are two viewing terraces. No rush though. Everyone's going down to see the geyser first and then hobble back up here to buy the local crafts. If we do the opposite, we'll beat the crowd."

The open-air marketplace rumbled with motion and noise. Tourists cluttered the path and stalls, merchants hawked their regional crafts, hot grills slapped with meat threw out pillows of spice-seasoned smoke to temp the crowd, and the air clogged with voices—shouting, haggling, begging, gossiping—in dozens of languages, mostly Spanish. Dust kicked up by thousands of feet mingled with the aroma of the very near ocean. Li went into sensory overload.

David led his friends through the stalls, charming the locals in their own tongue and getting a few freebies for his troubles. Li ran his fingertips over the soft skin of a leather bag, the plush of a hand-loomed blanket, and the smooth chill of a Mexican silver pendant. His heart ached that he couldn't afford just one little present for his mom. That blanket would have been perfect. She could snuggle up in it when it got cold enough to galvanize her arthritis.

Li glanced at the price tag, and the slim pleat of bills in his pocket howled with laughter.

Maybe I can buy a postcard for my collection, he thought. *I might be able to afford that.*

And the searing spurt of jealousy he felt when he saw Travis unload his bank account for a leather belt didn't help either.

"Okay, we did the girlie stuff," David said, "now let's do the manly stuff. I know a guy here that sells some really premium tequila. If we play nice, he'll give us a taste."

Travis slipped on his new belt. "All right! That's what I call service! Let's get...Oh shoot! What are we going to do with Mr. Clean-and-Sober over here?"

Both heads turned to Li.

"You guys go ahead," he replied, trying to smother the wave of jealous sickness he felt as he watched Travis admire his purchase. "I want to explore on my own for a bit. Maybe go down to the geyser."

David nodded. "We'll meet there then. Now remember, Patrelli, this is only a taste. Not that you can afford a bottle after paying for this ridiculous belt and that crazy buckle."

Travis played with the buckle, trying to make the sunlight bounce off it and around the stall. "Hey man, it draws attention to my best asset."

Li stumbled into the crowd, woozy with budding depression, and hoped to find a postcard stand where he could bankrupt himself. Someone fell into step beside him.

"Nice to get away, isn't it?"

Li jumped and stared into the face of Rosemary Hale.

"Mrs. Hale?"

She laughed, and Li noticed how the stress lines around her lips were nearly invisible. "I'm sorry! I didn't mean to scare you. I just wanted to talk."

"Talk?" His mind groped for the most pessimistic outcomes. *Does she want to talk about Charlegne? Did she hear that stupid rumor too? What if someone sees me talking to her? What will they say about that? And what will her husband do? Is he jealous? Why does this always happen to me?*

"Yes, silly. Talk. I missed you at the Captain's Table last night. I told Jean Paul that I wanted you to serve our table, but I gather he's part of the problem." Her smile seemed warm and genuine, but Li couldn't suppress the memory of her mutation into the Dragon Woman. "Come on. Let's sit down at a table and chat."

She hooked him by the arm and pulled him toward a stall selling blankets and *serapes*. The colorful woven draperies rustled in a mellow breeze, sunlight ferreting out the hidden jewels in each hand-dyed thread. It was an altar of rainbows.

"So," she said as they settled at a wooden table, "what's your name?"

"L-Liam."

"Well, Liam, tell me about yourself."

Li wrung his hands together so hard that his knuckles burned white. "H-How come?"

Rosemary tilted her head to one side and studied him. She pushed her sunglasses to the top of her head, and her emerald eyes sparkled with encouragement. There wasn't a ripple in the milky smoothness of her complexion.

"You look like you have a story tell. I saw how close you were to a nervous breakdown. And it worried me. So I thought I would ask around."

It was all bundled up inside Li. The pain...the fear...the sickness...He stuffed it inside his heart. His mouth quivered. He dug his teeth deep into his bottom lip. No one needed to know how hurt he was, how angry he had been, and how badly he wanted to go home.

Rosemary warmed his cold hand with hers. Something about the glow in her eyes and the tenderness of her voice reminded Li of his mother when she would talk to him after he was bullied at school. Her questions were gentle; her face expressive of a genuine compassion that tugged at the battlements around his heart. And wasn't there an echo of grief in those green eyes? A grief that seemed to mirror his own?

She asked the question Li both wanted and feared. "What happened to your dad?"

Li broke. His eyes started to leak. He made a soft whine like a hurt dog. Then words, broken and wet with tears, flew out his mouth.

"He was my best friend. Dad and I were pals since I was a baby. He used to make my mother insane with worry, because he'd take me to construction sites and have me in a playpen in his office with wooden toys he made for me. Dad took me everywhere. I was his boy. Everyone knew what I meant to him. And he was my Papa! He knew everything about the world! I used to pester him for hours with questions about everything from why the sky was blue to why Mom spent so long getting dressed in the morning. Sometimes he laughed—It was a great laugh, one of those husky ones that always feels warm when you hear it—but he would answer every last question I had. And he was honest. He never lied to me, and he never kept secrets. I knew how taxes worked when I was ten! Dad...Dad liked that I was so curious. He said it meant I was smart. And I used to tell him everything about what happened at school or with friends. I could trust Dad."

Li stopped to fist the tears from his eyes.

"He loved to build things. It was more than his job. He just loved to put things together. When I got interested in medieval stuff in kindergarten, he made me a castle out of cardboard. And I don't mean a refrigerator box with windows cut in it. He spent days fabricating this huge structure with turrets and chambers and places to hide. I loved that castle. Dad and I spent HOURS playing in it. Sometimes he'd be the scary dragon, and I'd be the knight who would save the kingdom. Sometimes we were both knights on a quest to find my mom's good silver, which Dad always hid. Mom would often force me to go to bed, but Dad would always wriggle out a few extra minutes of playtime. I think he had more fun than I did." Li sniffed, and his face scrunched up into a strict knot to keep the tears from falling. His voice cracked. "And I was forced to throw it away after he died!"

Rosemary paled, and her own lip trembled. "How did he die?"

Li lifted a shaking hand and raked his fingers through his hair. His stormy-blue eyes, the same color as his father's, swelled red. "I was fifteen. We all knew he wasn't feeling well. I didn't worry about it. Dad would tell me if something was wrong. Dad told me everything. We had no secrets." He laughed, but it was a short, sharp noise that hurt his throat. "Well, it turned out he researched his symptoms and got a diagnosis long before he told us! He never mentioned seeing a doctor! Not once! He had been terrified of telling us, his family, that he was sick and dying. That's how he put it. At dinner one night. While my little sister talked about her class trip to the aquarium. The four of us just sat around the dining table, eating my mom's tuna casserole, when he blurted it out. 'I'm dying,' he said. That's all he had to say! 'I'm dying.' Then my sister started to whimper." Li stood so abruptly that one of the textile rainbows slunk to the ground in fright. "And I was furious! How could he not tell me, his son, that he had leukemia? We never had secrets before! How could he keep that from me? And how could he just drop a bomb like that and not give us any warning? To this day, I can't even look at tuna casserole without wanting to puke!"

Li saw the sharp glint of fear in Rosemary's eyes and sank back into his chair.

"And then I was angry at myself for being angry. The man was dying from leukemia. It had to be hell for him to try and explain to the family he adored that...that he was going to get very sick very fast. And that there was no cure. Do you remember 9/11, where all those families were ripped open by one big smack in the face?" Rosemary nodded, white to her lips. "It felt like 9/11 in my heart. I felt like some monster, some lunatic, murdered my Papa and I stood there and watched. It wasn't enough that I had to hear about it. For two years, I had to sit and watch him die. When my dad told us he had leukemia, my childhood died. And my baby sister, who was only twelve at the time, had to hold her Daddy's hand in the hospital while he tried not to bawl in front of her!"

Li cried then. He collapsed into his folded arms and bawled, his sobs loud and rough as they scraped their way out of his body. Rosemary squeezed his arm with a delicate hand. Her voice was soft, encouraging. "It's okay. Let it all out. Don't hold back. I'll know you better if you do. I...I understand how you feel."

His words were muffled. "I didn't make the most out of those two years. Everything was a haze. Sometimes I avoided seeing my dad. I know I shouldn't have. But I couldn't stomach the idea of seeing the man who would move the earth to make me happy lying crumpled up like a used tissue in a hospital bed. He just got so weak. That hurt the most...to see him so helpless."

Rosemary's eyes started to flood with tears. Her words stuttered a bit. "There you go. Keep...Keep talking."

Li lifted his head. His face burned with tear stains. "It was expensive. When the housing market crashed several years ago, my dad's business went belly up. He had to shut it down. Then...Then the leukemia. We sold so many of our belongings to pay for whatever relief we could give him. The TV. Christmas decorations. Furniture. Anything we could lay our hands on! That's when I took on my first job, to try and pay my dad's medical bills. We wanted doctors there. We wanted them to think of something. We didn't care that there was no cure for this disease. We wanted them to make a cure!" He was hysterical now. His shiner flushed black. The altar of rainbows trembled in a new gust of wind. "And none of it worked! We couldn't save him! I couldn't save him! Why couldn't I save him? He was my Dad! He did everything for me! Why didn't I try to do this one thing for him?"

"Stop," Rosemary said, her voice weak and wavering. "Stop right now. You did everything you could possibly do for him. He wouldn't blame you."

Li stopped screaming, but he still wheezed and whimpered. "I blame myself."

"Don't. That's the worst thing you can do. He loved you. He wouldn't want you to suffer like this."

Li looked out at the laughing, smiling bustle of people. His stomach churned. "I'll always suffer. He died two years after the diagnosis, which is unheard of in this form of the disease. I was seventeen. Just a kid, really." His eyes dropped to his dirty, threadbare sneakers. "We were broke by then. We couldn't afford a funeral. We held a memorial service in the backyard. Our neighbors paid for a cremation. My dad's ashes sit in an urn on our mantle."

"You didn't think to spread his ashes?"

Li jerked his head back and forth as if any undue motion would unleash more tears. "No. Dad was already taken from us. We couldn't bear letting him go a second time." He wiped his nose on his sleeve. "And my luck has been rotten ever since. I could only afford to go to a community college, if I worked my butt off. Well, the State budget put so much strain on the college that they cut classes I really needed. I couldn't afford to go to school anymore. So I dropped out. But I still try to study on my own, because I know that's what my dad would want. Then it got too expensive for all three of us to live at home, so I volunteered to move out to spare my mom and sister. I haven't seen them in months." His wet, swollen, hurting eyes flicked up at the woman seated across from him. "Well...that's my story."

Rosemary dabbed away her loose tears. Her stress lines returned, cutting dark lines into her skin. "Next time, warn me that you're going to break my heart."

"I'm sorry, Mrs.—"

"Oh please, don't be sorry! I asked for it. I just didn't realize..." She cleared her throat. "I know how you feel. I...I also lost a loved one in...in a really horrible way."

"You mean Dustin?"

It was a fatal mistake. Li wanted to bite back the words the second they escaped his lips. He saw her nostrils flare and her pupils contract. He thought about diving under the table to dodge the explosion.

Rosemary lifted her hands as if warding off the charge of fury. "Normally, I want to butcher anyone who so much as mentions my baby

137

brother, but I think you've had enough trouble in your life. How did you learn about him?"

"I...I accidentally overheard your fight with...with your husband."

She seized a lock of flaming hair and started splitting it into individual strands. "So, you heard all about how my husband wanted to sleep with a murdering bitch, huh?"

"Oh, I don't think that—"

"So now you're an expert on my husband? I've been his wife for twenty-two years! I know when he wants sex! And I guess since I can't get pregnant, he'll—!" The words caught in her throat. Tears bloomed in her eyes. "Damn it...I should have known that would hurt."

Li rested a tentative hand on Rosemary's own. "You...You're infertile?"

"That's the polite way of saying it. Marty and I...we...we came on this cruise to try and escape everything. It...It was HELL knowing that I couldn't have a family of my own. It...I...Well, maybe I should start from the beginning."

She began twisting the loose curl of hair into a tight coil. Li noticed how hard her throat worked to keep the sobs down and the way her eyes darted to his face. At that moment, he felt connected to her and her grief, to the long years of suffering they both endured. They both lost people they loved. They both lived with the guilt and pain day after day, constantly reminded of what they lost. They both wanted nothing more in the world than to escape the past. He could see his feelings and fears mirrored in her anxious glance. He squeezed her arm for comfort, worked to keep his own raw emotions in check, and spoke as calmly as he could.

"Go on. I'm listening."

Rosemary swallowed her sobs, her voice quivering. "My brothers and I were orphaned as teenagers when our parents died in a car crash. We were the last ones in the family. The rest were dead. So we went to live with friends." Her eyes misted over with memories. "They were nice, but they weren't family. They had their own kids to worry about. It was lonely. So my brothers and I became inseparable. We formed our own little family." She chuckled, but it was a hollow sound. "We used to call ourselves the Three Musketeers. All for one and one for all. I would have killed for my brothers."

"And Dustin?"

"Dustin…" she whispered. She stopped coiling her hair and throttled her purse handle in her fists. "Dustin was a sweetheart. He was only fourteen when our parents died. My big brother and I raised him through those really tough years. I was worried that maybe he'd grow cold and distant, but not my baby brother. He still knew how to love. He had a huge heart, open to everyone. He loved with his entire soul." The dragon flashed on her face for a heartbeat. "And then that bitch destroyed him."

"Charlegne?"

She threw him a poisonous glare. Li recoiled from what could turn into another strangling. "Is there any other slut evil enough?" Li chewed on his lower lip. Those venomous snake eyes narrowed. "What? Is there something you want to say? Do you disagree with me? But I guess all men are biased where certain blondes are concerned." Her grip on the purse tightened until her knuckles popped. "Well, Liam?"

"I thought she was an unhappy woman."

Whatever Rosemary expected, it was not that.

"Why the hell should she be unhappy? It's not like she lost a baby brother to suicide! Suicide she caused, by the way! She had everything in the world! She was a damn queen even when she took a dump! And all she had to do was kill my brother! What did she lose?"

Li recalled Charlegne's words during that first dinner.

Anything you lost isn't nearly as bad as what I lost…

"I think she lost a fiancé."

A vein pulsed in Rosemary's temple. Again, Li noticed the strain her throat went through to suppress the screams scratching against her lips.

"And you think she loved him enough for that to make a dent in her flawless life? Obviously, you don't know the whole story of what that pretty, perfect whore did to my family." She bent toward Li as if ready to drop hot gossip into his lap. "Charlegne modeled for my line some sixteen years ago, back when she was the biggest name in couture modeling. Dustin helped me out backstage during shows. That's where he met Charlegne." Her eyes slipped into the haze of memories again. "He couldn't fight whatever spell she put on men. He adored her. It was sweet at first. Dustin was horribly shy and tended to blush when she floated near him. And when you have red hair, blushing is not becoming. But Charlegne seemed charmed by it."

"Did…Did she love him too?"

"It seemed so at first. Charlegne was a different woman then. Open. Friendly. Very smart. Had an eye on her future. She studied fashion design at FIDM. She wanted to start her own line before the gilt came off her modeling credentials." Rosemary's brow pleated in a frown. "I'm sorry to say I helped her. She was like a sister to me. I thought she loved my brother. She had the decency to blush whenever I asked about him."

"Sounds like true love."

"I thought so. They seemed perfect for each other. My big brother was a little jealous of them, in fact. At the time, his girlfriend left him after an ugly fight, and he was still sore about it. But there was never any hostility toward Dustin and Charlegne."

Li's mind taunted him with a less sentimental approach. *I think there would be a little hostility. To see someone in a happy, healthy relationship after losing your own is enough to make anyone jealous.*

Rosemary's eyes hardened into brightly polished spheres of malachite. "A year after they met, they were engaged. I was...I was thrilled when it happened, because, you see. I had already designed Charlegne's wedding dress. I had accepted her as a sister in my heart. She was family to me. I thought...I thought she would make Dustin happy."

"But what happened? Why wasn't it a happy ending?"

Rosemary's defenses against her temper were pulling apart at the seams. Conscious of the crowd just outside the stall, she hissed through bared teeth. "The stupid slut left him for another man!"

Li could see, in her heavy breathing and the determined thrust of the bones in her face, that they sat on the razor's edge of Rosemary's suffering. He could not provoke a woman who had lost her brother, her hopes for motherhood, and possibly her husband's love.

"I can't see why she would leave a man who loved her," he said, measuring his words with extreme caution. "Your poor brother."

A tear crawled down her cheek. "He was heartbroken. He called me when it happened, bawling his eyes out. She sent him a letter saying that the engagement had been a mistake, that it shouldn't have happened in the first place. Then she disappeared. She deserted Dustin. It was too much for him. He never really recovered from Mom and Dad's deaths and losing another person he loved was like driving nails into his heart. So he...he..."

Li covered her hand with his again. "You don't have to tell me."

"No…No, I want to…" The stiff ridges of bone in her face seemed to melt with her tears. "He killed himself…threw himself off a bridge not far from his apartment. It was an awful scene. My big brother and I got letters from Dustin, and when we got to the bridge…" Her eyes, troubled with memory, widened, and her hands were rigid claws protruding before her as if she cradled her dead brother's head. "The blood was all I saw. All on these huge rocks under the bridge. I bet that's why he chose that bridge. The blood…the blood was everywhere. There was a big smear of it. The officer at the scene said that…that Dustin hit the rocks and bled to death. Then gravity pulled his body down the rocks, smearing the blood, and he fell into the river. To this day, I still picture his body. I cried every night for a year after his funeral."

Li felt his stomach twist in protest as he pictured the product of the suicide. A body broken by rocks, bloody from his wounds, and bloated from the river. "And Charlegne never learned about his death?"

Rosemary's words sharpened into ice. "Oh, I made sure she knew. She murdered my baby brother. She drove him to kill himself and then ran away with some asshole who left her the minute he got wind of her crime, I'm sure of it. She never modeled again. I didn't confront her until she started her line and we became rivals." The ice started to rumble with half-restrained thunder. "I let her know that she deserved to die. Painfully. I wanted her to suffer like Dustin. It wasn't fair that she lived while I had to bury my brother."

"I understand that you would feel that way, but—"

That was enough to ignite the powder keg. She screeched at Li, her face as red as Dustin's blood, her hair alive like fire.

"I hated her! I loathed her! I never forgave her for slaughtering Dustin! Don't you dare ask me to give a damn about her feelings, you son of a bitch!"

Li retreated from the blast, knocking over the *serape* display and sending a kaleidoscope of them sailing into the crowd. The merchant shrieked Spanish horrors at the boy until he caught a glimpse of the violent workings of Rosemary's face. He backed away, grumbling under his breath.

The interlude seemed enough to congeal her fury. Li's brain screamed for diversions. "Do you still have that letter from Dustin?"

Again, Li caught her off guard. Rosemary's eyes clouded with suspicion. "What makes you think that I kept it?"

Li bit his lip and said a quick, selfish prayer for his safety. "Well, I noticed the way you were clutching your purse earlier. You practically strangled it. And, no offense, you seem like the kind of person who would keep certain mementos of her painful past as...well...as 'reminders.'" He cringed, expecting a second explosion.

There seemed to be a boxing match under Rosemary's skin as her feelings fought wars on her face. One moment cold fear, the next implacable fury. She settled into a neutral expression that Li feared more than her rage. She opened her purse, withdrew a sheet of paper, and handed it to Li.

Rosie,

I know you love me, and I also know you won't understand this, but I can't think of another way to get rid of this knife in my chest. I keep thinking of the accident that killed Mom and Dad. When Lena left, it was like she died too. I love Lena. I'll always love her. Or at least, I'll love her for a little while longer. Please don't try to stop me. It will only make things harder to accept. I'm not as strong as you are. Never forget me, Rosie. Take care of our family. It's all we have left.

Dustin

"Family," Rosemary croaked. Her eyelids sagged with fresh tears. "You can imagine how this killed me for years. I've spent most of my adult life trying to rebuild my family. Charlegne was like a cancer. She poisoned any dream we might have had. She killed my baby brother. Martin and I found out that I was infertile. And my big brother's wife has a form of uterine cancer that makes it very unlikely that she'll have kids. So you see? Poison. I would be ecstatic that she's dead if she hadn't done so much damage already."

"What about adoption?"

Rosemary studied Li again, this time with a searching glare that pierced him. She unloaded a sigh and fingered the colorful fringe of the nearest blanket. "I thought about it. But somehow it didn't seem fair to the child. Don't get me wrong! I would adore a baby, no matter what. But, it doesn't seem right to bring a child into a house of suffering."

Li kept his thoughts to himself.

"I suppose you'd want to see this, too," Rosemary said. She dug around in her purse and handed him a crumpled ball of paper. "I found this in the trash can in Dustin's apartment. It...It's the letter she wrote to him. I kept it with me, because...I'm not really sure why. Maybe as a reminder, like you said."

Li's eyes dropped to the letter.

Dustin honey,
This is going to hurt so much, I know it. I'm sorry. I need to go away. It shouldn't have happened. I can't stay here. I need to put my life back on track. I've found someone who can help me do that I have to do this. I feel horrible even as I sit here and write this letter. I'm so sorry. I wish love was enough to fix this. But it's not.

I'll always love you,
Lena

"It almost seems like she's the one committing suicide," Li replied, returning the letter.

Rosemary crumpled it up and shoved it into her purse. "I don't give a damn about how she felt. She should have been honest with Dustin. She's a tramp for leading him on like that. Nothing will change my mind that she was the one who was morally responsible for my brother's death." She flashed him a withering glance. "And you saw what she became. Selfish. Self-entitled. Cruel. Nothing less than a hag and a bully."

A thought flared in Li's head. *A bully?*

"But she's dead," he mumbled. "Your husband told you that, didn't he?"

"Why? Do you find that interesting? Yes, Marty told me that Charlegne died. From sunstroke, I hear. Well, that's poetic justice. After all the years I had to put on a happy face when we were in public...after forcing myself to adopt a stupid sunny disposition when I felt like ripping her face open with my fingernails, Charlegne's the one who got burned. In fact, you could say she's..." She chuckled, but it was cold, sadistic. "...sunny side up."

Li shivered. The July sunshine felt as cold as December.

Rosemary stood and perched the sunglasses on her face, closing further discussion. "I'm only glad I wasn't alone with the bitch. If that ever happened..." Her smile was as friendly as Aaron Brent's. "...I might have greeted her like I did at Fashion Week last year."

Li walked toward the geyser, dragging his feet and rousing a thick cloud of dust at his ankles. His head felt stuffed with cotton. His plan had been to die with his guilt and grief, to never buckle, to never let the ugliness around him shatter his illusion of self-control. And, in one afternoon, his disguise had been stripped away. He had vomited his suffering to a complete stranger. The hunger to go home and beg forgiveness at his father's ashes plagued him like the aftershocks of a nightmare.

I feel physically ill, he thought. *My stomach won't stop writhing. Why do I feel like I betrayed Dad? He knows how this guilt is killing me. Getting it out of my system should have helped. But I keep remembering what I did during those last two years. Why didn't I see him more often? Why couldn't I be a better example of what he taught? Oh, my stomach...*

Li wrapped his arms around his midsection and prayed away the sickness.

Then the earth roared.

Li stumbled over his own feet, his eyes desperate to locate the source of the explosion. Blinded by the naked glare of the sunlight, he could make out certain sounds. A cluster of shouts. A rumble of brittle thunder. Something wet sprinkled on his face, and his stomach rebelled.

Then his eyes scaled the hundred plus feet of a roaring tower of water.

"You're late."

A man with purple-dyed hair and matching eyebrows thrust a jumble of shoes into Li's unprepared arms.

"Don't you dare drop these Manolos," Purple said, his Continental accent thick in his throat, "or Ratface will be on your ass like Lycra hot pants. Now get these on Kennelly's feet before I hear that stupid little whinny of hers one more time."

"But I don't—"

Purple cut off the protest by stomping towards an elaborate photographer's set-up down on the terrace. The model's petulant whine rose over the tumult and moaned about the heat, the tourists, and the bellowing geyser, a violent contrast with her dark, brooding, Katharine Hepburn looks. Li, cradling the shoe cluster like an abandoned child, jerked his head in every direction.

"Whoopsie."

The new voice was cool, amused, and pressed a cold spot into the nape of his neck.

Priscilla materialized at Li's side and squeezed his arm with her gloved hands. Her hat served as an umbrella against the sunlight, drowning her in shadow. Her smile was more at home with nannies placating fussy babies. With a lilt in her voice, she called out to the crowd at the photo shoot in unctuous French. Purple strode to them, treated Li like a misplaced coatrack, and ferried the shoes down himself.

"My apologies," Priscilla said, maintaining her grip on Li's arm. "Sebastian must have thought you were one of the styling assistants. Silly mistake. But I was hoping I'd have a chance to talk to you."

Li cocked an eyebrow. *Does everyone want to have a heart-to-heart with me now?* "You were?"

Her smile reminded Li of a loaded pistol. "Yes. Why don't we walk for a bit? The sea air is too refreshing to miss. Come along."

"What about your photo shoot?"

Priscilla shrugged by tilting her chin to one raised shoulder. "It's only a little cover shoot for *Harper's Bazaar*. Jean Claude is an artist, and Sebastian can handle Kennelly Richards better than her parents could. I won't be missed."

She hauled Li toward the edge of the terrace, her fingers like a vise on his upper arm. Li realized she had no intention of letting him go.

"I just want to say how brave it was for you to find poor Charlegne, yesterday," Priscilla said. "That's not easy for children to experience."

"I'm twenty."

"Yes, yes, but still a child to many. Like your poor parents. It must be torture for them to know their baby boy is out here alone, working like a servant and feeling terribly homesick."

"My mother handles it just fine, Ms. Reilly."

Priscilla's cardinal-red lips pursed into a prim smile. "And your father?"

She stuck her pin right into Li's heart. "My...My dad died when I was in high school."

"Oh, you poor boy..." She drew a gloved finger along his jawline. "So brave. So *young*." She pulled down on his bottom lip as if inspecting his gums. "And not a bad face either."

He could see the way her amber eyes traced his features, calculating the geometry of his face with expert precision. Li felt panic flood his body as her smile widened with each passing second.

"Such a handsome, lonely boy," she cooed.

"W-What do you want from me?"

"So many people loved Charlegne. It's a horrific tragedy when someone like her...well...exits the stage so soon." Priscilla changed her tone from panther on the hunt to sympathetic event planner. "We're going to host a special memorial for her. Just a few old pictures and dresses and things like that. But the important things are the stories." Those amber eyes glowed as she pulled in her prey. "Imagine it...Standing before the fans, the loved ones, the people ready to mourn the beauty lost to us all... the lonely boy with eyes like a lake in the rain remembering his poor, sweet father's untimely demise. A catch in his throat...the slight puddle of tears against his lashes...he recalls discovering the body of a woman he had admired for many years, a beauty so senselessly destroyed by a jealous Mother Nature. The boy sobs...it is painful to remember violence against beautiful souls...those of his father and the woman he admired. He is the face of grief, and tears leak from the lakes of his eyes, an image for history, the icon of loss and love." She gave him a very arch grin. "It would be selfish not to share your story with others."

Her hands staunched the circulation to his fingers by now. Spellbound, Li could barely croak out an answer. "You want me to be the face of your 'We miss Charlegne' campaign?"

The tiniest frown line puckered between her eyebrows. "Don't you think that's an irreverent thing to say?"

"I do. It fits with this whole idea of yours."

Priscilla sighed lavishly and looked out at the sea. La Bufadora roared to life again. She didn't turn to look at him when she spoke, but her voice had a businesswoman's grit.

"Material or moral objections?"

Li stopped trying to wrench his arm out of her grip. "Excuse me?"

"If it's money, *La Charlegne* can provide a VERY generous donation to you and your family AFTER services rendered. If it's more than money..." She flicked a hand at the photo shoot. "...there will be dozens of girls like Kennelly who will want to meet the charming face of the boy so broken by his dad's death. And with my help, we could put this face to more profitable use." She glared at Li, her pale honey eyes burning. *Ratface*, Li thought. "I can make something out of you. You're not the tallest or in the best shape, but we can work with that. A few weeks at the gym, a good diet, a new haircut, and *GQ* will be kissing your ass to get you on the cover. Eyes like yours don't come around that often. Don't waste them."

All this because of my eyes? No...All this because she wants to use me as a marketing tool.

"I don't think you can give me what I want."

"Try me."

He could feel her fingernails through the glove now.

"Bring my dad back to life."

Priscilla's eyes withered into slits. She watched him closely. Then her face smoothed into a sneer, and a chuckle wormed its way from the cave of her throat.

"I should have known. Moral objections. The impossible price. You ask for something I can never give you. Listen, kid..." She tugged him under the shade of her wide-brimmed hat. "I don't give a flying rat's ass about whatever goody-two-shoes morals your Daddy spoon-fed you when you were a little brat. They don't work outside of La-La Land." She permitted a light snarl to touch her top lip. "Sometimes, you have to do things you aren't proud of to get somewhere in life. Morals are for children's stories. There will be times when you must do something a shade off-color to get what you want." She turned her glare to the unbothered horizon. "I didn't become the head of *La Charlegne* by being a saint."

Li knew both of his parents would yell at him for being so rude, but he couldn't block the insulted, rebellious words boiling in his mouth. "And all it took was Charlegne's death, right?"

Priscilla snapped her head back at Li, her eyes animated with fury, a panther scenting danger. They soon cooled into an expression of bland interest.

"A tragic accident." She stressed the word. "Totally unforeseen. Of course, it was a shock, but Charlegne planned for any eventuality. She decided years ago that if she were unable to continue heading the line, I would be the most logical choice as her successor. Naturally, her death has been heartbreaking..." And here, she looked as heartbroken as a hungry crocodile. "...but her wishes were set long before this cruise. She would have wanted me to shepherd this label with confidence and skill. I am only a servant to her wishes."

If Li hadn't already been on such a raw, emotional tightrope, he might have staved off his tattered temper. But some hotheaded and injured imp inside him wanted to claw the evil satisfaction out of those amber eyes.

"You still haven't found that bottle of sunscreen, have you?" His tone was cold, sharp, intended to wound.

Priscilla didn't conceal her boredom. "A trifle. A zealous admirer pocketed it as a souvenir from the lady he adored from afar. It happens."

"But Charlegne wouldn't forget to use sunscreen, would she? She wouldn't refuse protection from the sun, right? *Because there was no sunscreen on her skin when we found her.*"

He wanted to see fear. Or guilt. Even just a flicker would do.

What he got was a glint of surprise.

"I am not in charge of what my employer chooses to—"

The silvery-blue of Li's eyes gleamed like the blade of Excalibur. "But she DID use it. Someone SAW her use it. So where did all that sunscreen go?"

Her grip hardened on his arm, and his fingers tingled with oncoming numbness. She had every desire to hurt him. Li fought to keep from wincing. It was astounding how her iron muscles could be so efficiently cloaked by designer fashions. But a steel beam gilded with gold leaf remained steel.

"I don't have a clue what you mean," she hissed, "but I am totally blameless. I never saw her that day."

Li's memory blazed into life. "Not even when you ordered her breakfast?"

Priscilla's dainty nostrils flared. "No. I ordered it from my cabin. I always knew what she wanted. I didn't need to bother her and..." Her eyes glittered. "...whatever she may have been doing."

She knows something, he thought, but before he could ask, she continued on the outline of her innocence. "I spent the afternoon on Catalina Island in the company of two women, Daphne Cole and Sally Brent. They'll corroborate everything. We went to a little dress shop, a drug store, and the Casino. I had only been on the ship for a little over an hour before I got the news about Charlegne."

She thrust her chin toward him and closed the inquiry.

Li wasn't easily dissuaded, now that the volatile imp in his heart found the perfect pin to burst her bubble. "That's strange, Ms. Reilly. I thought Charlegne would want you at her side all the time. Wouldn't she?"

"That's none of your business!"

"But if you had been there, you might have been able to save Charlegne's life. But you weren't there!"

The ghost of his father rose in his mind, shaking his head and frowning. *That's a low blow, son,* he said. A spasm of guilt broke the boy's glare. He dropped his eyes to his feet and begged his father for forgiveness.

Priscilla unclamped her hand from Li's arm. There were tiny slits in the fingertips of her gloves from where her nails poked through the fabric. Anger frayed her voice. "It wasn't my choice. Charlegne wanted to be left alone. She told me so the night before." She sat, ankles crossed, on the edge of the concrete terrace, glowering at the rocky crags clustered among the waves. "I went to her stateroom before dinner to settle the itinerary, choose her dress for dinner, and so on. She told me to handle the business with *Harper's Bazaar* on my own and gave me the afternoon off. I went to Catalina Island, and she stayed on the ship." She shifted her scowl back to Li. "This wasn't a bizarre request for her. She often asked Steven and me to leave her alone for the day. After all, this was her vacation."

She rose from her seat like a queen preparing to give a proclamation. Her face was set with aristocratic finality. Her eyes, narrowed but burning, remarked that all discussions were closed. She turned back to the photo shoot.

Li's inner imp had the last word. "A vacation that ended in murder. I think you realized that, Ms. Reilly. Someone murdered Charlegne."

Priscilla wheeled around and punched him in the face, making sure to use the hand with the most rings. Li flinched as her fist came toward him, and got clocked right between his nose and his cheek. Another centimeter and she would have crushed his nose. He stumbled backward.

Priscilla's golden eyes glittered while she watched blood spout from the boy's face. "I don't know what the hell you're trying to suggest, kid, but you're an idiot. Your father didn't teach you much. I'd like to see you try to squeeze an admission of my guilt out of Sally Brent's innocent eyes. Any further discussion will go through my business manager, Steven Danforth. Don't you dare speak to me alone."

She marched off with the grace of a Prussian general and howled at her staff.

Li tried to curb the nosebleed with his hand. The wounded imp mumbled a few sailor-tongued oaths that he would speak to her business manager and it wouldn't be pretty.

Then the watery blue eyes of Sally Brent bubbled to the surface of Li's brain.

He knew them. He recognized that haunted stare constantly on the threshold of tears. He had seen it before. Where? He dredged his memories, trying to skim over ones that included his dad. A headache blossomed at his hairline.

A pair of hurt, desperate, tear-soaked eyes.

The headache eased. His eyebrows climbed his forehead.

He knew where he saw Sally Brent before.

And it came right out of his high school past.

CHAPTER 17

Bullies

"At least your nose isn't broken," Travis said, piling a full henhouse of fried chicken onto his plate, "although listening to Doc's lecture on horse-play left me feeling a little busted. I still think you should talk to someone about Princess Priscilla's right hook."

Li's eyes glowed with uncharacteristic greed as he followed Travis's lead on the chicken. "No use now. She'd just deny it. And I stopped bleeding hours ago."

"Hey! Aren't you pigs going to leave some for the rest of us?" Lusty French oaths crowned the complaint.

Travis gestured accordingly and took half of the mashed potatoes for himself. "I can't believe she socked you just because you wouldn't be her poster child. Although maybe you should have stuck with that modeling contract...I mean the babes alone—"

"Wasn't going to happen. Priscilla would promise me anything to get me to agree to her plan. But she'd wriggle right out of those promises like the Ratface she is."

Travis smirked. "I'm glad to see you both left on friendly terms."

"Who took all the mashed potatoes?" This was followed by a multi-national uproar farther down the line.

Li, satisfied with his plate, slunk out of the queue. "You know everyone is going to lynch you for your appetite."

Travis looked a little depressed that he couldn't fit one more roll on his platter, but he followed his friend. "If they aren't used to it now, they never will be. And don't think you can get off so easily, buddy. If only David was here to see you eat something mildly unhealthy for a change."

No eloquent comeback could hide Li's blushing. "Shut up, Travis."

"Guess you used up all your big words on Ratface Reilly." He plopped down at a table, chuckling. "Man, I'd love to shake the hand of the guy who came up with that name. Pure gold." His smile sagged. "Although seeing you clutching a bloody nose and looking like your dad rose from the grave and popped you a good one is enough to take the shine off the memory. What happened anyway?"

Li stopped detaching the crisp skin from a chicken thigh, but his eyes never lifted from the plate. "I...I remembered something and...I wondered whether it's important enough to tell someone."

"Is it about your dad?"

"No."

Travis's grin brightened a few thousand watts. "Now I'm interested. So will you spill or is this going to be another tooth-pulling?"

"I don't think I have the energy to argue with anyone."

Li rolled a free swatch of chicken skin into a tube and used it as a spoon for his mashed potatoes and gravy. One bite and all his muscles relaxed. The meat may have been good, but fried chicken skin had been Li's guilty pleasure from childhood. He never missed a chance to have it. Crispy, juicy, spicy...it warmed Li's body like a hug.

"You're stalling, Li."

He took another bite, savored the secret spices in the breading, and swallowed. "I remembered why Sally Brent's face was so familiar to me."

Travis turned his attention to his own pound of poultry. "An old topic, though I guess learning about your secret obsessions is a sacrifice I make for friendship."

"Well, when I was a senior in high school, I dated this girl—"

"Whoa! Hold it! Don't tell me you dated Sally Brent? She would have been twice your age then! Isn't that a felony?"

"Would you let me finish?"

"Will the story be more interesting if I don't?"

Li popped him on the arm with his fist. "No. And stop interrupting. Normally, your mouth is too stuffed with food to do anything else anyway."

Travis grinned, but kept quiet.

152

"Anyway, during lunch, I met this girl behind the band room. I'm going to call her Melanie." Travis's forehead puckered and the tips of his smile sank. "Melanie was one of the friendliest people in school. Ran several clubs and volunteered for nearly every school event. Then, shortly after Homecoming, she withdrew from everything: friends, clubs, school. She became a shell. When I met her behind the band room, she had been cutting her wrists with a razor blade."

Travis's smile died like a blown light bulb.

"She was terrified that I discovered one of her secrets. I wanted to take her to the nurse. Melanie refused, said she knew what she was doing. She took out all these first aid supplies from her backpack and started to bandage herself up. I insisted that she had to see the nurse or a counselor. She said she would sooner kill herself than see them, told me not to tell anyone what I saw or she'd come after me, and then bolted into the parking lot."

"And you ended up dating her?"

"Not for a while. You see, after school, I saw her walking home. I decided to walk with her. I told her that I didn't feel right about hiding her problem from people who could help her. She called me stupid and said I didn't know half of her problems." Li's guilty pleasure started to cool in his hand. "We argued. I worried that she would end up in a morgue someday. My dad died the summer before, so I was constantly afraid that everyone would die around me. Melanie eventually broke into tears and dragged me off the sidewalk to the parking lot behind the ice cream parlor and told me what happened to her."

"Jesus..." Travis whispered. His face was gray with dread.

Li was the definition of discomfort now: hands tearing apart his chicken, eyes shifting from corner to corner, voice weak and hesitant. "Well, her date to Homecoming wanted to have sex with her after the dance. She refused. So he took her to his house and raped her."

The oath Travis muttered was the most colorful Li ever heard.

"That's how I felt too. I couldn't believe some asshole did that to her. But he did. And ever since, she had been plagued with nightmares and felt him crawling under her skin. That's why she cut herself. To 'get rid of him,' as she put it."

Travis looked at his plate, and his face suggested that the idea of dinner disgusted him. "What did you do? Did you get the police involved?"

"I wanted to. The minute I heard 'rape,' I wanted to dive into the ice cream shop and phone them. But Melanie refused. Apparently, I was the only person she told about what happened that night. And she had no intention of sharing it with anyone else. Not her family. Not her friends. No one. She just wanted all the memories to fade away."

"And let that pig walk free? Why didn't you make her call them?"

Li gave Travis a hard look. "She threatened to kill herself the moment she heard anyone asking about that night. What could I do? She was on edge. If there was even a hint that the police were interested, she'd end her life...and end their case. I wanted to try and coax her into agreeing with the police plan. Slowly. She was in a volatile state. If I pushed her too hard..."

He left the rest to imagination.

"But what did you do?"

"Talked to her every day. Acted friendly toward her. That's what she needed. A friend who knew and understood. Eventually, I started taking her on dates. I think she enjoyed them. She even smiled a few times. Once, she kissed me." He gazed at the wreckage of his meal on his plate. "Then she broke up with me after six weeks."

Travis slammed his hands on the tabletop, earning a full harvest of scowls from people around them. "Wait a minute...She broke up with you? Why?"

Li shrugged. "Maybe I did push her too hard. Maybe I should have left her alone. But I really wanted to help her. She was like a damsel in distress." He poked at his cooling chicken. "I know that sounds sexist, but I couldn't stomach the idea that I saw her cut herself and did absolutely nothing to help her. I had to do something." A sigh pushed out of his throat. "She made all the stereotypical girlfriend excuses. Some days, I think she cut and pasted together phrases from other break-up letters to make one for me. I...I cried and tried to fight for our...would you call it a relationship? I cared about her. I let myself care about this girl who had been hurt so badly."

"Are you sure you should be telling me this?"

"Wouldn't matter anyway. A week after she broke up with me, she hanged herself in the girl's locker room. In one of the old shower stalls."

There was a pale green flush to Travis's face. "I will never ask you to tell me anything that happened to you ever again." He pushed his food away with his finger. "But how did that make you think of Mrs. Brent?"

"I thought you weren't—"

"Just shut up and tell me."

Li flinched, but, since his friend looked ready to ralph the dent he made into his food mountain, he complied. "It was Sally's eyes. Or more the look in them. They were haunted, abused, hurt. It hit me. The same look was in Melanie's eyes when she told me about her rape."

"So what does that mean for Sally?"

Li slipped out of focus again.

"Do you think Aaron Brent is the kind of man who would maritally rape his wife?"

The green flush filtered out of Travis's cheeks. He drew his eyebrows together in a frown.

"No, I don't."

Li didn't contain his surprise. "Really?"

"Yeah. I know he's an evil son of bitch, but I got the impression that he thought he owned his wife. Like she was a favorite piece of furniture or something. I never got the impression that he found her interesting sexually. Or that he saw her as anything but his wayward daughter. Every time he hit her, I bet he believed it was nothing more than spanking a bad child. But I don't believe he'd rape her. That's too intimate."

"Strangely enough, that makes sense. She's nothing more than property to him. And that makes how he treats her even more disgusting." He took a bite of his now cold chicken. "And it begs the question: Why did they marry in the first place?"

Travis forked through his own meal. "Maybe she's got money. Since he's obviously trapped in ancient, chauvinistic views about women, maybe he thinks a wife will bring him prestige and a positive image. Especially a wife with money. And he abuses her to keep her modern thinking in check."

"But why on earth would she marry him if they don't love each other?"

Travis left that question alone, so the two friends ate their dinner in dour silence. Li's stomach argued against the cold food and unhappy memories. But he had to eat something before service, so he bullied himself into swallowing a few bites.

Bully. The word simmered in his brain. *A bully's crime.*

Light glimmered in his eyes like a sunbeam through storm clouds.

"You thought of something," Travis said, pausing in his renewed attack on his feast.

"Rosemary Hale called Charlegne a bully."

"Sounds accurate. Although she wasn't as big a bully as Powerhouse Priscilla turned out to be. What about it?"

"You said that taking the sunscreen was nothing more than a prank and I just wondered..."

"What?"

Li imagined a shadow slicing across the unconscious woman and a tempted hand grazing a bottle of sunscreen resting nearby. "...if it was the sort of prank a bully would do."

Travis steepled his fingers and tossed a sidelong glance at his friend. His generous mouth pulled into a taut slash on his face. "I wondered about something too, buddy."

Li squirmed. He didn't like the dark suspicion churning in Travis's eyes. A very skeptical imagination toiled behind that curious gaze.

"What is it?"

Li knew in his bones that his friend brewed some sort of scandalous idea about his conversation with Rosemary. Could he help it that fashion designers took a shine to him? Li armed himself for war.

Travis folded his hands and prepared to judge the damned again. "Why did you talk to Rosemary Hale?"

A headache drummed against the roof of his skull.

Why am I always getting in fights? Can't I have an hour where nothing happens?

Li's latest argument with Travis succeeded in splintering their friendship again. Travis believed there was too much evidence against Li to fully trust in his innocence. Li countered with a less gentlemanly response. Li sought more solitary adventures in his free time before a late dinner service.

He knocked on the door of the Security Office.

A thick, lazy drawl welcomed him. As he stepped into the room, he had the instant impression of strolling into some super-secret command post for the CIA. A wall of monitors, blinking with black-and-white pictures of every corner of the ship, provided the backdrop for a large, semicircular desk bulging toward the door. A man with a weak attempt at a mustache reclined in his chair, propped his feet on the end of the desk, and grinned at his guest. His nametag said IAN.

"What can I do for you?"

Li's eyes darted from monitor to monitor, shivering at how watched they were on the ship. He could see Paul in the crew mess draining mug after mug of coffee, sobering up for service. *Ian can see everything.*

"You got something to say to me, kid?" Ian asked, jolting Li out of his thoughts.

"Oh...um..." *Crap, I didn't think this through.* "...just...uh...seeing if anything happened recently." He swallowed painfully. "Seems quiet."

Ian's idle grin never faltered. "Sure is. Clean as crystal. Nice and quiet."

"You didn't...miss anything? Like with one of the passengers? Charlegne, perhaps?"

The smile stayed, but a calculating scrutiny flickered in his eyes. "I miss nothing, kid. I'm down here all the time. Got a slight sensitivity to fragrances. Plays hell with my asthma. And these ladies like to bathe in the stuff, so they put me down here. I'd run out of medication in my inhaler if they didn't. I got a relief officer to cover the night shift, but I'm here every day of the cruise. And I didn't see anything happen." A lewd spark winked in the corner of his eye. "More's the pity, eh?"

Li shuddered. The man's certainty was cold, final, but he openly suggested that something had happened and he was upset about missing it. *A voyeur,* Li thought.

A second cursory check of the monitors revealed that no cameras were found in passenger or crew cabins.

"Is that it, kid?"

An idea sparked in Li's head like a burst of light from a flash bulb. "Could I see the Lost and Found box?"

It was a long shot. What if the bottle of sunscreen wasn't thrown overboard? Since Ian claimed that he saw nothing out of the ordinary, what if the murderer—Li was steadfast on that belief—simply took the sunscreen with him and abandoned it somewhere on ship? Then a crew member would turn it in to Lost and Found. That way, the cameras wouldn't catch him throwing the bottle off the ship.

Ian slipped a clipboard out of a drawer. "Did some bullies take your lunch money?" He handed the clipboard to Li. "Policy's changed. No one can simply look in the box and take what they want. We catalogue the items now, so you tell me what you're missing, and I bring it to you."

Li scanned the list. It was staggering what people can lose on a ship: a few silver bangles, dentures, some instant-picture camera, a wrap dress, a single slipper, a Rolex, a bottle of nail polish, swim trunks, a white bathing suit, a pair of leather pants, and a pack of cigarettes.

No bottle of sunscreen.

"If you haven't found what you lost, I'll take the clipboard back now. And I won't take the box out to see if I missed anything." His smile slid into a sneer. "I miss nothing, remember? Besides, something stinks in that box, and I'd rather save what little of my lungs I can."

Ian snatched back his paperwork, dropped it in the drawer, and used his heel to close the drawer. The voyeuristic glint kindled, then blazed, in his eyes. He dragged a red tongue over dry lips. It felt like X-rays speared Li's body.

He can't ask about that stupid rumor. He sees everything! He saw me leave after I delivered her tea that night! He would know I never went into the cabin!

Then the feeble, unwelcome voice of reason reminded Li about the night relief officer. Ian didn't watch the monitors that night. He learned about the rumor like everyone else.

Ian traced the line of his half-assed mustache with his tongue again. His eyes glowed with expectant pleasure at details he was unable to learn through his profession.

"So what was she like in bed?" he drawled.

Dry flakes of burgundy sauce melted in the flood of soapy water, revealing the golden sheen of the plate. Li settled into his pattern of washing dishes. Tonight hadn't been so bad. Paul and Mr. Brent had nursed twin wine headaches and could only manage a surly growl or two. Li reveled in a peaceful service. He even found himself enjoying the usual kitchen rush. Though there was that one disturbing comment from Jeremy about finding dirty pictures in Li's quarters.

He's bluffing, right? He didn't find any pictures in my bunk, dirty or otherwise. The only one I have is in my wallet, and I'm never letting anyone see it.

Slipping the dish into the rinse water, he decided to just enjoy the silence. He could let his wounds heal. No Paul. No customers. No new injuries. He was blissfully alone. Even his thoughts were cheerful. His lips bent into a small smile. He began to hum a few bars of a favorite Queen song.

He stopped before the chorus. He only hummed when he was totally at peace with his surroundings.

Somehow, this made every nerve stand out in bright, white relief.

He shook out the thought and resumed scrubbing.

His head snapped up. There was an alien sense of intrusion—of someone breathing his oxygen. Li jerked his head toward the doors. A silken rustle of air…a quick patter of tiptoes like the velvet paws of a cat… the tingling sensation of pressure against his personal space.

He was not alone.

Li wound his fingers around the handle of a soap-soaked saucepan and raised it in defense. His breathing started to sprint. He inched toward the locus of pressure, creeping, the suds drooling onto the floor. His ears strained for the flimsiest sound.

A slight whistle of metal…pots and pans sliding against each other… the intruder doubled back to the drying racks. Li felt his heart in his throat. What was he thinking? What if this was the killer? All he had was a half-clean saucepan for a weapon. He should have escaped through the kitchen doors. He would have been safe then.

Unless the intruder meant to hunt him down.

Another bump, this time nearer the sink.

Li held his breath and charged toward the noise, swinging his opportune weapon like the bats he swung in Little League. The intruder threw herself against the wall and collapsed into a knot of noiseless terror.

"Mrs. Brent?"

Sally crossed her arms over her head and batted away the blows that would not come. Her hands were rigid like arthritic claws. Li dropped the saucepan back in the sink and tried to soothe her wild, lurching panic. He didn't have the heart to admonish her presence in the kitchen. She was punished enough.

"Mrs. Brent, it's okay. I'm not going to hurt you. You just caught me off guard. I'm sorry if I scared you."

A wide, blue eye poked out from under the scaffold of her arms.

"I promise I won't hurt you, Mrs. Brent." A new realization flooded his brain. "And I promise not to tell your husband that you were here."

She's alone, he thought. *She managed to escape her husband. Does he know where she went? And how long before he finds out?*

Li stretched out a hand and helped Sally stand. She creaked to her feet as if her joints needed oiling. Her face cowered behind a greasy sheet of pale hair.

"Are you all right?" Li asked.

She jerked her head downward, then drew it up slowly. A nod.

"May I help you?"

Her hand, stiff with bone, grazed his cheek. Her voice, heavy as a falsetto, hobbled over her tongue.

"D-Did he h-hurt you?"

Li brushed his fingertips over the swatch of purple fattening in the crook between his cheek and nose. "Oh no! No, this was someone else. Your husband never laid a finger on me."

Sally wrung her split ends like a wet towel. "But he does want to hurt you. It's the same game."

Li felt his skeleton shudder. "Game?"

Another rusty nod. "Just like the bellman at the Champagne Shores Resort."

Now he felt like a ghost sailed through his body.

Sally wrung her fingers, the nails torn by teeth. "They're always so young, and they need their jobs badly. Aaron...Aaron makes it hard for them. H-He has a nose for the one in the most danger of losing everything." Her lower lip shook. "He never physically hurts them, but...but sometimes there's an accident..."

Accident. Li thought about the incident that earned him his second strike with Paul. Something that read on the surface as Li's mistake.

His ankle tingled with the memory of contact with a foreign foot.

Tears dribbled through her lashes. "A bellman might lose control of his cart...A junior stylist might slip and nick a person's ear...A waiter might trip and fling food at someone..." She pushed back a ream of fair hair. "And these poor kids can't prove Aaron did anything! They get hanged for it! Their bosses sacrifice them! I have to sit and watch them, on their knees, begging for their jobs. But it never works. We often find them in an alleyway or a homeless shelter several months later."